About the author

Jemma Hall has worked as a copywriter and administrator for several years whilst harbouring a dream of becoming a novelist. Lunch breaks spent in her car, feverishly scribbling words and chapters in a notebook, have finally culminated in *Cocomolioco*, her first novel.

Jemma lives in North Yorkshire and enjoys exploring her home county on the search for weird and wonderful trees.

COCOMOLIOCO

JEMMA HALL

COCOMOLIOCO

Pegasus

A CIP catalogue record for this title is
available from the British Library

ISBN-978 1 91090 381 0

*Pegasus is an imprint of
Pegasus Elliot MacKenzie Publishers Ltd.*
www.pegasuspublishers.com

First Published in 2023

**Pegasus
Sheraton House Castle Park
Cambridge CB3 0AX England**

Printed & Bound in Great Britain

Dedication

For those who wander

For those who wonder

Acknowledgements

To Graham, for his love and patience through countless evenings when I couldn't resist scribbling "just one more paragraph" in my notebook.

To Mam and Dad (Meg and Tony), for encouraging me to be no more and no less than who I wanted to be.

To Hayley, for her generosity of spirit.

Prologue

This could have been a story about a woman blissfully and elegantly following her dream of opening a chocolate shop.

It could have been a story about warm liquid chocolate swirling over cool marble surfaces in mesmerising figure eights at the expert flick of a palette knife.

About the sprinkling and stirring of delightful additions to enhance the host mixture, the dipping and flipping of truffles, the slicing of gianduja, the cracking of praline, the crumbling of honeycomb.

But a grouchy ghost called Patricia intervened — and it all became a lot more complicated.

Chapter One

In the time it took for Magnolia Aitken to walk from one end of the High Street to the other, she'd progressed from considering the purchase of some pleasingly pointy shoes to the absolute decision she was going to buy a chocolate shop instead.

Well... it wasn't a chocolate shop yet; it was an empty husk tacked on to the end of the High Street that had previously been a pizza takeaway shop. And she wouldn't be buying it properly, she'd be buying the lease — if she was the successful party. These two things were inconsequential, though. The point was, her itchy spirit was finally about to be scratched. She was often given to flights of fancy, but this was no such thing; it was felicitous and wholly inevitable.

Peering through the windows, she saw that the unit comprised a shop at the front, with a small kitchen at the rear. The shop space had just a basic counter running along the back, separating it from the kitchen; obviously where the till had been and where the freshly cooked pizzas were placed for collection. Any other furniture or fittings had since been removed, and all that littered the glorious wooden floor were a few dancing dust bunnies.

She considered the delightful possibilities. After twelve years working in an accountancy job (which paid the bills but didn't allow her to be even slightly creative) and now armed with a plump redundancy package plus inheritance from her grandmother, her imagination was running wild. How many different chocolate treats could she showcase within this space? Should she go all-out with a dreamy décor to match?

She could envisage shelves lined with elegant boxes in rich jewel shades of ruby, emerald and sapphire for the most sophisticated chocolates; cheerful drums and tins for the chocolates more appealing to children; cute little cellophane packets and bags dressed with satin ribbon for the occasions when just a little soupcon of indulgence was sought.

She imagined a smattering of customers inside — adults and children alike filled with wonder and relish at the choice to be made; adults tapping their children's hands away discreetly as they reached for their chocolate desire.

Oh, and the scent on the air! There'd be an exquisite fragrance of hot chocolate laced with zesty orange or comforting vanilla (she really must try to install a hot chocolate counter) as well as freshly toasted almonds, lavender fondant, Jamaican rum ganache and flambéed banana from the kitchen beyond.

Adjoining the empty shop to the left was a delightful artisan bakery; the exterior of both properties the same beautiful buttery brickwork. As the High

Street was a muddle of buildings in different architectural styles, some much more attractive than others, this pleased Magnolia greatly.

To the right, the street curved around the corner for thirty metres or so, before coming to an understated solicitors' office.

There was no accommodation above the empty shop, which was disappointing in one regard, as Magnolia quite liked the idea of living above her *chocolaterie*; but at least it meant no one else would be in too close proximity.

As a passer-by cast a curious glance towards her, she feigned nonchalance and strode away, ridiculously paranoid that they too were considering taking on the shop. She waited until they disappeared before going back to take a photo of the leasing agent's contact details with her phone.

Walking on, she came to her brother's bike shop. She paused and peered in the window. If he was just pottering around, she wanted to share her momentous decision with him. Unfortunately though, he was checking the frame size of a bike against a tall woman in alarmingly tight, white jeans. She threw her leg out as she mounted the bike, almost kicking Mark in the face in the process (he was crouched down, making an adjustment to the pedals) and Magnolia felt thankful she hadn't knocked on the window to draw his attention.

Taking a deep and delightful sniff of the fragrant potted yellow roses by the doorway (courtesy of her green-fingered sister-in-law) she moved on. She now had second thoughts about speaking to Mark at this point, anyway. He might try to dissuade her. Better to make the all-important call to the agent first and get things moving.

Between the High Street and her terraced townhouse was a lovely little park that she frequented. Whilst not big enough for a run or a walk that she could class as "proper exercise", it was perfect for a wonder-filled wander beneath the oak and beech trees, or a half hour or so reading on a bench by the duck pond. It was the place for ideas and decisions, for wallowing and for healing.

This was her destination for making the telephone call requesting an appointment to look at the vacant shop — she really didn't trust her courage to last the walk home.

Dipping into a quiet spot by the hydrangea patch, she paused to take a restorative breath. The close-fitting bodice of her sundress, the unusual heat of the early summer's day and the fizz of excitement in her belly were making her sweaty under the arms; ridiculously, she felt she shouldn't be making a business call in a less-than-fresh state. As if they'd somehow pick up on it at the other end.

This was also a chance to make her parents truly proud of her. They'd said countless times that they were proud of her, but she felt quite unremarkable compared with her brother; who had set up a successful cycling retail business from scratch, accomplished various mammoth cycling challenges and proved himself to be an all-round charming chap. Plus, he and his amazing wife had now given their parents a wonderful granddaughter.

All Magnolia had done with her life was move numbers from one column to another on spreadsheets and faff around with chocolate in an ad hoc manner. She couldn't seem to find a boyfriend who ultimately didn't irritate her, and she had no desire to have any children.

Not that she was jealous of Mark; they got along with each other wonderfully well, and his close physical presence if she really was to take on her own chocolate shop — being just across the road — was yet another factor in favour of the leap. It would be lovely if he popped in for a coffee and a chat every now and then — his wry observations on random situations always lifted her mood.

Pushing these notions aside, noting the excellent phone signal, she nervously dialled the agent and held her breath.

Six minutes later, it was done. 'Yay!' she exclaimed, jumping on the spot with excitement. A self-important drake looked at her haughtily before crossing her path to the female ducks beyond. 'Oh, don't be so snooty.' She addressed his waddling backside ridiculously.

Grinning widely, she pocketed her phone and went home for a bath followed by tasty *burrata bruschetta* and a head full of wonderful ideas.

It therefore came to be that Magnolia found herself standing on the other side of the glass within thirty hours of having first cast a glance into a tantalising future. Smoothing the lapels of her smart summer tweed suit jacket, she looked the agent squarely in the eye and declared, with as much confidence as she could muster, 'I'll take it.'

She felt like the leading character in a film.

She felt like she was going somewhere she wanted to be.

The agent looked a little scared — which in retrospect, Magnolia would realise, was the first bad sign. Under the illusion it was her fierce attitude causing his reaction, she quietly rejoiced in her rebirth as "successful and formidable businesswoman", shook his hand and tried to pretend she wasn't looking over his shoulder to determine whether her desired hot chocolate counter would fit into the space behind him.

Their business done for now, the agent returned to his office feeling somewhat guilty. Whilst new business owners seemed (to him at least) to be getting increasingly younger and more annoying, Miss Aitken definitely had a particularly endearing mixture of naivety, steeliness and creative sparkle about her. He really didn't want her to meet the same end as the previous two leaseholders, but he hadn't been able to see any way of warning her off. Mulling it over as he ate his lunchtime cheese and pickle sandwich at his desk served only to give him raging indigestion and a keyboard full of crumbs.

'Well done getting rid of that hot potato on the High Street, Michael!' a passing colleague said, giving him a congratulatory slap on the back.

It seemed he wouldn't be able to forget the transaction any time soon.

Back at the shop, a blackbird touched down on the lichen-speckled windowsill of an outbuilding on a scrub of grass beyond the kitchen door. Peering at his reflection, he shook out his feathers — surprised that the bird in front of him did the same. Not as surprised as he was a second later, though; for there was a sudden shifting of shadows from within the outbuilding, before a great 'Raaaaaahhhh!' caused him to take flight in fright.

Patricia Daventry, satisfied that she'd yet again made her presence known, albeit to a lowly blackbird, cackled manically as she returned to her favourite corner to resume her dark thoughts.

Chapter Two
Bruges, twelve years previously…

Magnolia's dream of becoming a *chocolatier* began with an initially charming yet ultimately lacklustre fellow student on her university business degree course called Mathias, from Belgium — and gained in fervour in inverse proportion to her interest in him.

They'd been a couple for almost a year when they decided to spend the summer before their final year at university travelling Europe together — first stop: Bruges, where Mathias was born and where his family still lived.

As their taxi burred over the cobbles towards Mathias' childhood home, Magnolia marvelled at how a city could seem so magical, cosy and intimate; she was amazed that Mathias had never once enthused about this delightful place of his upbringing.

'Why didn't you tell me?' she whispered, clutching his hand in rapture.

'Tell you what?' he replied distractedly. He lightly shook her hand away so that he could tap on his phone.

'How enchanting this place is! The perfectly pitched roofs and turrets, the way the trees dip sleepily to the canals, the reflections in the water, the meandering cobbled streets with little hunchback bridges... the whole radiance of it!'

He looked at her agape. 'Calm down, Nolly. It's just Bruges.'

Moments later he was laughing quietly at something on his phone.

That was the first sign they weren't going to last much longer.

Mathias' parents, Agnes and Frederick, had a *crêperie* in the city centre with a little *chocolaterie* off-shoot. Instantly warming to Magnolia, they were keen to show her around the business on her first full day in the city — and she was just as keen to discover what they did there.

From the moment she stepped over the threshold and smelt the air — rich with warm chocolate and freshly made crepes, citrus, spice and caramelised sugar — she was captivated.

The following days fell into an easy pattern. Early in the day, Mathias accompanied Magnolia in exploration of the city. They climbed to the top of the belfry and rewarded themselves for the exertion with hot waffles and lashings of whipped cream (as if the view from the top wasn't reward enough). They visited museums; Magnolia relishing in taking her time whilst Mathias buzzed annoyingly back and forth like a trapped bluebottle. She delighted in seeing the famous golden Labrador gazing sleepily down at them from the foliage-lined open window of a bed and breakfast as they bobbed past on a canal boat. Then she gushed over the elaborate window displays of the bountiful chocolate shops lining the cobbled streets.

By early evening though, Mathias was itching to meet up with his old friends, to play video games and drink vast amounts of alcohol. This was fine by Magnolia — indeed, she felt a sense of relief and delicious anticipation as the time drew near — for it meant she could ensconce herself in the kitchen of Mathias' parents' *crêperie-chocolaterie* to learn their craft.

The *crêperie-chocolaterie* was quiet on an evening, having closed its doors to the public at five o' clock. Pushing open the forget-me-not-blue door, feeling the graceful swirls of the heavily carved wood against her fingertips, still warm from the day's sun, Magnolia would feel a sense of happiness whisper towards her as she entered. It was as though the space was imbued with traces of the joy that the day's visitors had experienced as they sliced into their delicate, buttery crepes elevated by intense calvados-drenched apples or refreshing mint-speckled strawberries and cream.

She'd stand there for a few moments, just drinking in the retained atmosphere. She imagined alongside the sights and scents the gentle waves of easy chatter and laughter, and the clink and chime of glass; Agnes and Frederick used charming etched glassware for both their crepe platters and hot drinks.

Then she'd enter the kitchen, where usually Agnes, but sometimes Frederick, would be preparing to make chocolates — having cleared and cleaned the *crêperie* side of things. She did try to arrive earlier, to help out with this, but usually she was just too late.

Whilst a lot of the chocolate shops in Bruges sought to create the most spectacular sculptures they could envisage, thereby giving their shop windows real wow factor, Mathias' parents were more intent on creating the best possible flavour combinations. Their finished chocolates were by no means visually lacklustre — they were elegant, neat and enticing — you just had to make the effort to get close enough to the window display to see their modest beauty; you'd be persuaded to make a purchase, and then you'd be rewarded above and beyond your expectations. Long-standing customers and patrons of the *crêperie* knew this.

After two evenings under one or the other of his parents' careful tuition, Magnolia could temper chocolate — the process of heating and cooling chocolate pellets to the exact temperatures required to create chocolate magic. After four evenings, she didn't even need the thermometer for the tempering — she could tell by the viscosity of the chocolate, as it swished luxuriantly over the marble work surface, whether it was at the ideal state to work with.

Mathias didn't understand, nor show the slightest interest in, her passion for discovering all there was to know about chocolate making. As the days went on, their connection weakened. One evening, sitting in a *brasserie* so renowned for its generous range of Belgian beers that the drinks menu was as plump as the food menu, they found themselves miserable and silent in each other's company. When a couple of Mathias' friends dropped in, it was a relief for Magnolia to be distracted from their fading romance by the men's exuberant chatter.

In direct contrast, Agnes and Frederick were a joy to behold as a pair. By day, in the busy *crêperie* kitchen, they somehow managed to be both dynamic and serene in demeanour and in action. Magnolia found it hypnotic the way they effortlessly danced around each other, each fulfilling their own tasks harmoniously alongside the other. They were kind and generous, firm and focused.

But they were also pragmatic. Magnolia had sensed their delight when she'd arrived with Mathias; she knew they'd taken to her and that they'd hoped she and their son would have a long-lasting relationship.

Magnolia also knew, however, that they'd quickly realised they were witnessing the decline of something that had never really been much of anything of worth in the first instance. This was accepted, and they nevertheless treated Magnolia wonderfully well.

At the exact moment the two weeks they'd planned to stay in Bruges expired, Magnolia was in the *crêperie-chocolaterie*, dipping strawberries into a huge vat of melted chocolate so expertly, she managed a whole crate load within the slim slither of time the chocolate gave a clean, glossy finish before it would cool to a thick, dull mess.

Meanwhile, Mathias was fast eating up the miles on a train to Paris. It was obvious they'd gone their separate ways.

Magnolia spent the whole summer in Bruges, working for Agnes and Frederick, and enjoying free board as a result. To offset the indulgence of the sweet treats she was now inevitably sampling in greater abundance, she began running part of the canal path from Bruges to Damme three or four times a week. Pleasingly flat and delightfully tree-lined, the run enabled her feet to establish a natural rhythm whilst her head filled with creative ways of demonstrating her new chocolate making skills.

As the summer rolled towards autumn, with a heavy heart she snapped back to reality and made the arrangements for her return to the UK and her final year at university. Watching the wonderful couple and the marvellous medieval city that had inspired her so much disappear behind her, she was suddenly struck by one word: a word of her own imagination with a mysterious, frolicking feel to it; a name that rolled off the tongue deliciously — the name of her chocolate shop, one day.

Cocomolioco.

Chapter Three

The day Magnolia received the keys to her new shop was an ice-cream and sand-between-the-toes kind of day. On the High Street, those without sunglasses squinted in the dazzling sunlight, and dogs with lolling tongues lapped at water bowls kindly placed outside the greengrocers and butchers.

'Nolly, you're an absolute fruit loop,' Magnolia's brother Mark declared, as they both stepped into the shop.

She'd asked him along for his opinion on the current state of the place, as well as her intended changes. He hadn't needed much persuasion — the alternative was yet another day at the beach with his wife and four-year-old daughter, and he'd had enough of tackling the chock-a-block coastal road this summer.

'Why?' she responded indignantly. 'What else would you suggest I do with my redundancy money and the inheritance from Gran? It's like it was meant to be. You know how long I've dreamed of being a *chocolatier*. And... you won't believe this... it cost nearly half what you paid for the bike shop.'

'You said that last night, but there's no way. That can't be right.'

Mark's brow furrowed as he took in the generous dimensions of the shop, his gaze sweeping over the sturdy oak floorboards, the perfectly plastered walls (which only needed a bit of a touch up), the space undeniably bursting with potential.

'So, I'm going to have shelving for the chocolates along this entire wall,' she announced, as she twirled delightedly across the floor and pointed at one of the side walls. 'I'm going to use old industrial water pipes as the shelf supports, or brackets, or whatever you want to call them, with planks of wood as the actual shelves. I'm going to see if I can source some chandeliers made from old water pipes, too; they need to be brass, copper or iron, though. I'm going with a steampunk interior design theme.'

'What's steampunk?' Mark looked alarmed.

'I've just told you what steampunk is. It's sort of industrial, yet romantic and quirky. It's a style inspired by steam engines and the Victorian era.'

Mark's alarm turned to enthusiasm. 'Ah, right. In that case you should buy an old-fashioned brass hot chocolate machine with loads of pistons and levers and weird gauges on it. That's if you're going to be selling your hot chocolate too?'

'Yes, absolutely! I'm going to have a hot chocolate counter with maybe four stools… right here… so that would be perfect. I need a huge mirror for the wall opposite the shelving, too. Do you think either you or one of your mates could get hold of a load of gears and

24

cogs for me? They can't look like bike gears, though; they need to look like gears out of a grandfather clock or some big old chunk of machinery. I want to glue them to the mirror frame.'

'What's in it for us? A lifelong supply of chocolate?'

Magnolia rolled her eyes. 'Nothing as generous as that — you'll put me out of business before I've even started. But I'm sure I can come up with some sort of goodie bag for anyone who brings me some top-notch craft materials.'

'Hey, what did Mum and Dad say?'

'About me opening a chocolate shop?'

It was Mark's turn to roll his eyes. 'No — about you having risotto for dinner last night. Of course, about you opening a chocolate shop!'

'Mum asked if it meant I'd be visiting them in Mallorca even less often, and Dad asked if he could escape here whenever they're back in the UK. When I told him that I was going to have a hot chocolate counter, he said he'd sit there and read his newspapers all day. He said it'd be an excellent way of avoiding Mum.'

Mark roared with laughter as he slapped Magnolia's clipboard down on the old pizza counter.

'Don't be putting that down — we have to-do lists to write. Come on.' Magnolia disappeared into the kitchen.

'Hang on, I need caffeine. And seeing as you don't even have a kettle here yet, never mind a fancy hot chocolate machine, I'm going over the road for takeaway coffee. Want one?'

'Christ Almighty, you'll do anything to get out of making lists. I'll have a large Americano, please.'

Mark left her nosing around, her head in the open pizza oven.

Unfortunately, Magnolia determined, the pizza oven had to go. Whilst quite a new and impressive addition, it plainly wouldn't be required for her future endeavours, and would just be in the way. She didn't even need the standard oven; all she needed was a hob and a fridge freezer. The generous storage space and expanse of marble work surfaces were perfect for her requirements; there was nothing she needed to be added, just a few things which would be best taken away. Thank God that was the case, for this was an assessment that she really should have made before taking on the lease.

With clipboard and pen, she set about making a list of priority tasks to be completed for the kitchen to be chocolate-making-friendly.

As the glorious day unfurled into a golden evening, Magnolia settled in her garden — doodling logo ideas, trying to sip a glass of wine as slowly as possible, and intermittently thinking she really should bring her recycling bin in.

The rumble of the bin's wheels down the driveway heralded the arrival of Mark. *Oh, great,* she thought sardonically. She didn't think she could take much more of him today; he'd grumbled throughout the whole recce of the shop.

'Don't worry, I'll bring your bin in,' he said with exaggerated weariness, depositing it in its usual place by the fence.

'Ta, bro. Grab a beer from the fridge as reward,' she replied, without looking up from her sketchpad. He disappeared into the house, returning a couple of minutes later with the suggested beer.

'Won't Claire go bonkers? You've already spent a couple of hours at the shop with me today, and now you've turned up here.'

'They're still at the beach.' He swatted her feet from the chair they were resting on so he could sit down. 'Anyway… I have important news. I know why the rent on your shop is so low.'

'Hmm?' Magnolia paused her doodling and pushed her sunglasses up her nose.

'Your shop. The reason the rent's so low. It's haunted.'

'Oh, of course — why didn't I think of that?' She laughed and took a sip of wine.

'Loads of people are saying so. I was telling some of the lads at the bike shop this afternoon that you'd taken on the lease and they told me all about what happened to Pizza Pizzazz. Didn't you wonder why

27

those guys suddenly just upped and left? It started with weird noises late at night whilst they were cleaning up after closing — unexplained footsteps and swishing sounds at first, but after a few weeks it got worse. A muttering voice... then loud bangs and clatters... objects started moving. Initially they thought they were just misplacing things. Eventually one of those heavy iron pizza pans flew right through the air from nowhere, nearly walloping the manager, in front of two other guys. Really crazy poltergeist shit.'

'Can you actually hear yourself?'

'Fine. Believe what you want. But don't be phoning me begging to be rescued when bowls of melted chocolate start throwing themselves at your pristine steampunk walls.'

'I'm not actually having "steampunk walls". The walls are just normal walls.'

'Well, whatever. You obviously don't want to take it seriously. Oh, by the way, I forgot earlier, Claire gave me a batch of mint leaves for you.' He reached for his jacket pocket and retrieved a plump paper bag heady with fragrance.

'Ooo, thanks.' Magnolia took a quick peek and stood up. 'I'd better put them in iced water.'

'She said: can she be cheeky and have a few once you've candied them?' Mark shouted, as his sister moved to the kitchen. The kitchen window opened, and Magnolia stuck her head out.

'Yeah, sure. What does she want them for? I can retain the leaf shape when I candy them, or I can make crystals.'

'She's baking a fancy cake for some school fete. She mentioned a fairy woodland theme — does that mean she wants the leaves intact?'

'Wow, not sure. I'd better ask her later. What's brought all this on?' Magnolia's sister-in-law, whilst a wizard in the garden, was not known for her culinary ambitions.

'Robo Bitch' Mark replied faux-solemnly.

'Who's Robo Bitch?'

'Well, that's the thing — I can't even remember her real name anymore, which is a bit of a problem when I drop Sophie at school. She's one of the other mothers. According to Claire she's a bitch, in a robotic kind of way. One of these days it's gonna accidentally slip out when I speak to her at the school. I've told Claire we at least need to shorten it to RB, so it's less likely she finds out.'

'Oh, it'll be Donna Drake, I reckon. I've never known anyone dish out insults in such a monotone. She does it in such a way that you end up wondering whether you heard her right.'

'That's her!'

'Hey, are you staying for dinner?' Magnolia's head popped out of the open window again. 'I've got fresh spinach and ricotta tortellini; from the deli on the High Street, though — I didn't make it myself.'

29

Mark screwed up his face. 'Nah, thanks. I can't be doing with vegetarian food today. Claire messaged me to say that they've just had fish and chips before driving home, so now I've got a craving for that too. I'm going to call in at the takeaway on the way home. Not as good as eating it beachside, but never mind.'

He stood up and approached the kitchen window, passing his empty beer bottle to Magnolia.

'I'll be off, then. Watch out for that ghost.'

'Yeah, OK. Watch out for rogue bicycle spokes poking you in the eye.'

Chapter Four

The bakery next door was called The Loaf of Riley. Magnolia had been well acquainted with the place when it was under previous ownership, but just a couple of months ago, the nephew of the retiring baker had taken over.

Magnolia thought the new name and shop exterior were utterly charming, and whilst she hadn't yet had the time and opportunity to form a firm opinion, from what she'd sampled of the produce so far, the quality of bread, particularly her favoured sourdough, was as good if not better than it used to be.

This morning she wanted to introduce herself to the new owner. She was keen to let him know that she wouldn't be selling cakes, only chocolates, so was unlikely to be competing with him for business.

She needn't have worried, though. Jed, as he introduced himself, nonchalantly told her that unlike his uncle before him, he didn't sell cakes anyway, and had no intention of doing so in the future.

Except *stollen* and mince pies at Christmas.

Indeed, his main focus right now, having already expanded the bread range to include several *focaccia* — most notably a thyme, wild garlic and parmesan one and a piccolo tomato and pesto one — was to look at incorporating vegetables into his loaves.

'What better way to get the kids to eat courgettes!' he said like a cartoon villain, rubbing his hands in a cunning manner whilst his kind, baby-blue eyes betrayed him as a big softie, really. One of his assistants gave a knowing and affectionate smile as she brought a tray of super-fresh pillow-like bread buns to the counter, and Magnolia caught the warm and nutty scent of caraway seeds that unfurled on the air.

'What's the coating on your sourdough bread?' Magnolia said; she'd been meaning to ask this for a while, and kept forgetting each time she came in to buy it.

'Semolina flour,' piped up a small voice beside her, matter-of-factly. She turned to see a boy, surely no more than six years old, waiting for his mother to pay for a couple of loaves. 'It gives it a lovely texture.' Magnolia was struck dumb by his knowledge.

'We love the bread from here,' his mother said, addressing Magnolia. 'I'm so glad that we found you,' she added to Jed, putting her purse back in her shoulder bag before picking up a larger shopping bag, plump with loaves. 'Nowadays Eddie actually eats his sandwiches. We used to get our bread elsewhere, but I couldn't stop him swapping his school packed lunch for dinosaur stickers.'

Eddie grinned.

'He's one of my best customers!' Jed said, laughing delightedly.

They chatted a little more, before Magnolia went onwards to her own shop, relieved that her next-door neighbour seemed to be a lovely chap.

Despite her bravado with her brother, she admitted to herself that she was quite apprehensive about entering the shop now she'd heard the rumours of a ghost.

Swinging the door open, she took a deep breath and cautiously stepped over the threshold.

Half-expecting a cold chill to overcome her despite the clement day, or a shifting of malevolent shadows from the corner of her eye, she was instead taken by a sudden surge of joy and excitement. This was her shop, a blank canvas from which her enduring dream would become reality. And the only shadows were those of the trees outside — patterns from their leaves and branches dancing playfully across the wooden floor from the window.

With renewed purpose she walked through the shop to the kitchen. Opening the radio app on her phone, the cheerful chatter of her favourite breakfast show flooded forth. The possibility of her shop being haunted hadn't entirely been dismissed from her mind, and this would help.

For the past few years, she'd been making chocolates in her much smaller kitchen at home. Whilst the extra space afforded by the shop kitchen was undoubtedly what she needed to progress her commercial enterprise, the initial excitement soon faded as she began to work. The fact was, it took more time to navigate from one work area to the next, and as she tried to multi-task by melting chocolate pellets whilst simultaneously setting out her shell moulds and extra ingredients, it became obvious that there would be a tricky transition period before she felt comfortable in her new surroundings.

There was also the difference in ambient temperature to contend with. For some reason she hadn't got to the bottom of yet, it was much warmer in the shop kitchen than she was accustomed to. And a too-warm kitchen was disastrous for chocolate.

Having started the day in a fairly relaxed mood — she'd kick-off the practical assessment of her new kitchen by making some simple ballerina-shaped solid chocolates for her niece's birthday — she quickly morphed into an irritable and irrational monster.

The chocolate wasn't cooling quickly enough after melting, and the ballerinas all had a grey-streaked, dull patina. Consequently, they were all thrown mercilessly into the sink, where they languished in various degrees of limblessness, reminiscent of some weird voodoo ceremony.

Time to start a fresh batch.

The same thing happened again.

'Oh, fuckkity-fuckarama!'

Patricia Daventry raised her substantial eyebrows and unfurled from her slouched position against the outbuilding wall. Her muscles and bones no longer needed the rest that such a position afforded, indeed no longer really existed, but habits are hard to break and she liked to pretend she was still human, anyway.

She approached the window and peered into the kitchen beyond. A young woman with delicate features and a precise knot of dark hair on top of her head seemed to be the source of the outburst. She thumped a bowl of what looked like melted chocolate onto the nearside worktop with such force that a few drops splashed onto the windowpane.

Patricia's gaze took in the rest of the kitchen. The young woman had certainly been busy. The stacks of cardboard takeaway pizza boxes she was used to seeing on the high shelf in the corner had been replaced by sacks of… chocolate? Cocoa beans? The packaging had French (or Belgian?) writing on it, anyway, and pictures of cocoa beans.

Instead of neat rows of Tupperware containing grated cheese and sliced onion, peppers, pepperoni and such like, there were now neat rows of chocolate moulds, all shaped like ballerinas. She must be trying to melt the chocolate before pouring it into the moulds. Surely that couldn't be too difficult? What was all the fuss about?

Then Patricia noticed that the usually shiny marble worktop running the full length of the back wall was completely coated in dried rivulets of chocolate. Was she pouring the chocolate directly onto the worktop? Why on earth was she doing *that?*

And anyway… how had all these changes occurred without her knowing? She'd always suspected that her stints of suspension in the outbuilding occasionally ate into the hours and days without her realising the passing of time, but during this latest stint away from the shop and kitchen she'd clearly missed some important developments.

Patricia moved away from the kitchen window and returned to the outbuilding wall, this time sinking to the ground and stretching her legs out fully, reminiscent of her long departed teenage self. She wished she could feel the playful tickle of the grass blades and their retained warmth against her legs; they would surely be warm — they glowed in the afternoon light as if they'd enjoyed several hours of the sun's splendour.

So… what should she do now? She'd successfully scared off the Pizza Guys, as well as the Shoe Fools (she couldn't remember the real names of their businesses — something bland and instantly forgettable). She should feel exasperated — that yet another stranger had taken on the lease of the shop instead of Nathan being tempted back — but instead she felt curiously sympathetic to Chocolate Girl. Did she really want to scare her away and ruin her fledgling business?

Chapter Five

As the summer days unfolded and Magnolia continued to work in her kitchen, a haunting more annoying than frightening ensued; such was the ghost's confusion over her changing motivations this time around.

Having made the blessedly small structural subtractions required in the kitchen for an optimum chocolate making environment, and discovering inventive ways to account for the different ambient temperature, Magnolia was now spending a few weeks honing her intended product range — alongside fulfilling several special commissions to keep her cash flow reasonable — before hopefully opening the shop in time for Christmas.

Magnolia's realisation that something odd was occurring began with the moments she'd get a little carried away with a song on the radio. Singing along unselfconsciously with one of her favourites, she'd suddenly hear a voice singing something completely different, ever so quietly in the background. She'd stop instantly and switch the radio off; there'd be a couple of seconds of the mystery voice continuing before it too stopped.

This went on for a few days.

Next, she was measuring up for the shelves in the main shop area, whilst considering the optimum quantity and range of produce to have on display, when she sensed movement in her peripheral vision. She quickly looked around; the tape measure snapping closed against her thumb. She was certain she'd seen a human shadow bobbing around the kitchen slowly and rhythmically, almost as if it was doing a waltz. Indeed, although it quickly disappeared once she looked at it, it'd been a little slow in doing so, and she caught a brief flurry of activity.

As time went on, increasingly there were unexplained shuffling noises and clicks; the noises a normal person would make if just going about their usual daily business, rather than the bangs and crashes associated with something more aggressive.

Then one day the ante was upped.

She was making honeycomb and had just added the bicarbonate of soda to the saucepan to create the foaming, lava-like magic, when a disembodied voice piped up, 'Looks like loft insulation to me.' Whirling around as quickly as she dared with blisteringly hot sugar on the go, she found no one there. The presence could no longer be ignored.

'You'll be wearing it soon!' she yelled, brandishing her spatula at the air, not sure where to focus.

She was met with unsatisfactory silence. A gloop of the hot amber mixture fell to the floor. 'Oh, thanks — look what you've made me do now. As if I haven't been doing enough cleaning and scrubbing already,' she grumbled. Quickly decanting the honeycomb into a flat tray to cool, she then shifted her attention to cleaning up the mess.

Afterwards, she'd look back on these extraordinary days with wonder over how she could have been so fearless. It was indicative of just how important her chocolate making was to her — to the extent that she hadn't even considered that her life might be in danger. Granted, she was well aware that something unusual was afoot, and the unpredictability of the paranormal performances were wholly annoying — but how had she not run from the shop screaming in fright?

The day went from bad to worse. By the afternoon, Magnolia was bone tired, irritated by the interference — there'd been a humming noise coming from the pantry for the last hour — and she'd just miscalculated the amount of ganache she needed to make truffles for an important commission, meaning she'd have to make an additional batch.

The guy fixing her shop fascia sign had been due at lunchtime, but he'd arrived late, been far too garrulous on his arrival, and she was worried he wouldn't finish putting the sign up before dark. She couldn't go on like this. It was too much to deal with.

It was time to meet the ghost head-on.

'Oh, for God's sake... this is ridiculous! I've worked far too hard to be scared off by some bonkers old ghost muttering and shuffling around and messing up my sodding ganache, so just tell me what the hell your unfinished business on Earth is, let's fix it, and then hopefully you can disappear in a puff of smoke or whatever it is you ghost-people do!'

Behind the pantry door, where she was trying to amuse herself by levitating a glass jar of macadamia nuts, Patricia's mouth fell open in a perfect O-shape, as a confusing mixture of admiration and indignation surged through her. The forgotten jar of nuts clunked back into their original place, wobbling precariously before settling.

Before she knew it, Patricia was standing on the kitchen-facing side of the pantry door. Chocolate Girl looked angry. And tired. And not at all scared to see her, though it seemed she *could* see her, judging by the challenge flickering in her eyes directly at Patricia.

'Can you see me?' she asked, needing clarification.

'Yes, as if by magic I can see you... now. Though I bloody well wish I couldn't.'

Patricia thrust her chest out and harrumphed. 'Well, then. You seem to think you know an awful lot about ghosts. You think it's that easy for me to cross over? Why don't *you* tell *me* what my unfinished business is?'

Magnolia rolled her eyes. 'Maybe when you were alive you annoyed the "Winner of the Most Tolerant Person in the World Award" or something, and once *they* become annoyed the whole of mankind is doomed until you put it right.'

'You have quite a weird intensity about you, don't you?'

'What! *You* try opening a new business that's way out of your comfort zone whilst simultaneously being haunted by a ghost who sings seventies rock tracks over and over in a tone that, quite frankly, is bad enough to curdle my ganache!'

'What's ganache?'

'*What?*'

That was the moment that Patricia discovered what ganache was, as a chunk of it launched from Chocolate Girl's hand and sailed through the air, straight through her body and onto the floor behind her.

'Oh, this is too bizarre.' Magnolia sank back against the kitchen work top, wearily. She took a proper look at the apparition before her.

The ghost woman was a remarkable example of neatness and decorum. Late sixties, average in height and build, she had an impressive waved bob of white hair; it swept back from her forehead and away from her ears in proud, luxurious swathes like a lion's mane. As though forcibly affected, it didn't move one iota.

She wore a plum-coloured silk blouse and the exact shade of plum-coloured lipstick to match. Magnolia fleetingly wondered if, had she chosen to wear a tangerine-coloured silk blouse instead, she'd have paired it with the same horrid tangerine shade of lipstick. Cream trousers and — not plum again! — court shoes finished the effect.

41

'So… who are you, anyway?'

'Patricia Daventry. I used to own this place when it was an antiques shop.' Patricia fluttered forward a little, then realising she was almost elbowing several neat rows of ganache — *You learn something new every day* — backed off a bit.

'And why are you here?'

'Well, that's just charming, isn't it?'

'It's a reasonable question to ask a ghost.'

'Don't ghosts deserve a little respect and humanity, too? Why don't you introduce yourself first?'

'Magnolia Aitken. Wannabe *chocolatier*.'

They eyed each other, cautiously and curiously, both wondering what to do next.

'Who are you talking to, the infamous ghost?'

Magnolia had forgotten about the signwriter, who now stood in the kitchen doorway grinning at his own wit. *Oh great*, she thought, *the whole town knows about the shop being haunted*.

'Do you want to come and look at the sign? It's in position, now.'

Evidently, he didn't need an answer to his first question. Magnolia glanced surreptitiously at Patricia; she was sticking her tongue out at him childishly.

'Let's continue this another time,' she hissed at her, then followed the retreating signwriter outside.

The breezy late-summer air was blessedly invigorating, and with a sense of anticipation, Magnolia delayed looking up at the sign until she was stood at a point on the edge of the pavement curb where she thought most passers-by would first notice it — she needed to experience it in this way for maximum effect.

'Oh, it looks perfect!' She clasped her hands together in rapture. Cocomolioco was written in a cursive font — almost like a swirl of smoke — white on a midnight blue background. She'd thought brown was too obvious and cliched for a chocolate shop, and whilst she wanted a slightly mysterious feel, black was too severe. Midnight blue had been the right choice.

Rooted to the spot, smudges of chocolate on both her apron and her pretty elfin face, she soaked up the moment; a moment that became rather prolonged for one passer-by, who cast her a curious look.

'It's my new shop,' she declared, proudly.

'Oh, right,' he responded, somewhat appeased. A few steps later he fully processed the exchange and turned around. 'Great sign. When are you opening?'

'First week in December, just in time for Christmas indulgence,' she replied, smiling engagingly. He responded with a thumbs-up and a smile as he walked away.

'Please can you take the ladder away now?' Magnolia implored the signwriter. 'It's spoiling it a bit.'

By the time she returned to the kitchen, the ghost had vanished.

Chapter Six

Magnolia felt herself hugged by fabulous roses that dipped drowsily towards her in a great curve — sat as she was on a sun lounger in a delightful alcove of Claire's making. Her sister-in-law had constructed a bamboo cane dome to encourage the fragrant blooms to cosy inwards, positioned two loungers and a small table within the space, and subsequently spent as many lazy, hazy summer hours luxuriating here as possible.

Magnolia was enjoying the mesmerising play of dappled light through the foliage as the somehow melodious burr of more than one lawnmower sounded in the distance. This backdrop of roses and suchlike would be perfect for a photo shoot, she considered, as she looked around in appreciation once again. If the shop became a success and she managed to build her online range too, she'd ask Claire if she could use her garden as the foundation for next year's summer promotional campaign.

Why on earth Claire wasn't interested in pursuing horticulture as a career, Magnolia couldn't fathom. When asked, she just replied vaguely that she didn't want to spend all her days wearing dungarees and dealing with slugs and woodlice. Being particularly sensitive herself about living up to the expectations of others, Magnolia had never pushed it.

She made a mental note to start looking out for vintage tea sets and swatches of fabric she could use as props, but decided not to jinx things by mentioning the idea to Claire just yet. She suddenly remembered that she also had a charming and regrettably under-used set of six Victorian custard cups — traditionally used to serve possets, mousses and such sweet delights at the end of a meal — with elegant curlicue handles that she'd like to incorporate into the theme, somehow.

Despite the serenity of Claire and Mark's garden, and her delight at her new shop signage, Magnolia's sense of relaxation was fleeting. Though she'd been determined to ignore it, her head started whirring again over the day's paranormal activity. A ghost was yet another unpredictable factor to add to the growing list of things that could scupper her chances of running a successful business; a colossal, uniquely peculiar factor that wasn't warned about in any of the textbooks.

Other than putting right any wrongs from the ghost's life, how could you completely get rid of one? If only her squatter was a vampire, instead. Then she'd just need a string of garlic, some holy water and a wooden stake.

Christ, was she really having these crazy thoughts?

'Oh, what am I going to do?' she sighed, bringing her hand to her forehead in mild distress. Momentarily lost in rapture at the lemon and rosemary truffle she'd

45

just tasted from the little sample box her sister-in-law had brought with her, Claire turned quizzically.

'About what, exactly?'

Magnolia's gaze wandered across the lawn to where her niece, Sophie, was carefully constructing a maze from grass and twigs for her pet snail. 'I'm beginning to think I was a bit hasty in taking on a shop.'

'Why? Don't let Mark and those ridiculous stories about a ghost put you off. It's the perfect next step. You've been making chocolates for us lot and for special commissions for ages; you've obviously got a real flair for it. And you've got a business degree, so you know what you're doing.'

'Yeah, but the smallest things are stressing me out. Truffles have always been my most popular item, but they're also the riskiest, 'cause of the short shelf life. They'll only last a few days, unless they have alcohol in them, like cognac or something — you know what happened at the harvest food festival, when I had to bin a load of them. So, do I play it safe and make a lot more pralines and solid chocolates, which last longer?

'And I can't even decide on the shop opening hours! Obviously, the longer the shop's open, the more I'm likely to sell, but I need time for making the produce as well, without being disturbed. My head is completely mashed.'

'Remember what I said. I'd love to spend a couple of hours a few days a week serving customers whilst

Sophie's at school. And you don't need to pay me, it'd be lovely just being in that environment.'

'You're an angel. I'll definitely pay you something, though... but the wage might have to be supplemented with chocolate.'

Sophie suddenly barrelled over excitedly, her garden-grubby starfish hands patting at the many loose blades of grass on the front of her citrus-coloured sundress as she approached, causing a flurry of them to take to the air around her.

'Mummy, I've had a great idea,' she announced grandly, after skidding to a halt before them.

'What's that then, sweetie?'

'I'm going to spray paint my snail maze in two-tone pink and purple... like my bike.'

'Absolutely not,' Claire responded firmly.

Sophie's lip quivered at the instant quashing of her creative dream. 'Why? It'll look really good!'

'Soph, just because we spray painted your bike, that doesn't mean you can spray paint everything.'

'Not everything — just my snail maze!'

Claire squeezed the point between her brows, exchanged a look with Magnolia, and then hunched forwards from her reclined position to address her daughter more clearly.

'Sweetie, it's really bad to spray paint grass — or flowers, or trees, or anything else in nature, OK? God made them that way on purpose. They're beautiful exactly as they are. Don't you think the grass looks

47

wonderful in its lovely natural green colour? Like emeralds?'

Sophie seemed to be considering this. Claire looked triumphant.

Prematurely so, it transpired.

Sophie cocked her head to one side. 'My teachers must be really wicked, then,' she determined. 'They've painted white lines on the school field so we can do sports.'

Magnolia snorted on a suppressed laugh. Claire cobbled together some white lie about the paint on the school field being magic paint, which grew increasingly rambling and tenuous, yet served to bore Sophie enough that she wandered back to her disappointingly green snail maze without any further argument.

'Phew, got off lightly with that one. Have some more tea.' Claire poured from the teapot without waiting for a response. 'Where were we? Oh, that's right — your sudden inferiority complex. Look, it's natural that you're nervous, but you've got the skills and knowledge to succeed — and your redundancy money now, of course, to top up the inheritance from your gran. What better way of putting it to good use? This is your dream, Nolly!'

A slow smile spread across Magnolia's face. 'It *is* my dream. Thanks for putting things into perspective, as usual.'

She popped a second truffle into her mouth; after her first failed attempt last week at this new flavour combination, she'd now managed to perfectly balance the woodsy depth and fragrance of the rosemary and the refreshing hit of lemon using a ganache base of half dark and half milk chocolate. Not too bitter, not too sweet.

That sorted, she now needed to shift her attentions to getting rid of the damn ghost. It was one thing pretending Patricia didn't exist to her family and friends — Patricia, for God's sake! What kind of name was that for a ghost? — but it was now starkly evident she could no longer pretend to herself.

Chapter Seven

'What on earth is that awful racket?'

Magnolia was grappling with her new hot chocolate machine in the shop when Patricia's disembodied voice next greeted her. She was beginning to think that all the fancy levers and gauges were more trouble than they were worth aesthetically. The machine was a refurbished model; apparently that meant it came with no operating instructions whatsoever. She could have sworn she saw a gleam in the delivery guy's eye as he presented it to her, as if to say: *Good luck trying to figure out the mysterious and wholly illogical workings of that brutish beast.*

'That's rich, coming from a poltergeist,' she quipped in return, flipping loose tendrils of wavy dark hair out of her eyes as she steeled herself for another investigation into the machine's devilish workings. It hissed, and alarmingly, wobbled a little.

Patricia floated over and without warning gave it an almighty wallop.

There was a moment of silence before it started to gurgle in a pleasingly productive way. As a steady stream of hot chocolate began to flow, Magnolia quickly placed a mug beneath the spout. It dispensed just the right volume and consistency, and they looked at each other with a shared feeling of solidarity.

'Wow, thanks!'

'Happy to be of service.' Patricia gave a comical strongman pose. They both laughed, and Patricia leaned in again, interested to see what was going on.

As Magnolia lifted the mug, a curl of steam rising from its contents, Patricia's jaw dropped in astonishment before dawning realisation crossed her face. She tilted her head back and sniffed deeply and joyously.

'What, can you actually smell it?' Magnolia asked incredulously.

'Yesssssssss,' was the blissful response. 'I couldn't smell anything before... but now it seems that I can!'

'Oooo, do you think you'd be able to taste it, too?'

'Don't be ridiculous. I don't have a body!'

'But yet you have an olfactory nerve. That just doesn't make sense. Obviously, you can see and hear things as well. How?'

'I don't know, do I? Just because I'm a ghost, that doesn't make me an expert on a ghost's key attributes and limitations.'

They both mused over the puzzle. 'Do I look any different?' Patricia asked.

'No,' Magnolia confirmed.

'I'm going to try something.'

Patricia swooped towards the open shop doorway... seemingly smacked into an invisible wall, and then fell in a heap on the floor. Her shape faded to almost nothing before her semi-transparent self was re-established.

'What just happened?' Magnolia was dimly aware that she'd slopped hot chocolate onto her wrist, as she felt the warmth, yet she couldn't take her eyes off the spectacle that was Patricia.

'I wanted to see if I'd be able to cross the threshold.' Patricia glumly returned to the hot chocolate counter. 'Since I became a ghost, I haven't been able to leave the confines of the shop. I can go as far as the garden out the back, where the outbuilding is, and as far as the shop front doorway, as you just saw. Now that I can magically smell the hot chocolate, I just thought other things, such as that, might have changed. Apparently not, though.'

'Can you feel anything? Such as launching yourself at the doorway as you just did... could you feel the impact? Or when you just bashed the hot chocolate machine... did you feel that?'

'No,' Patricia mused. 'Although... yes, I did feel a very faint connection; it seems to be only when I'm hitting something with a lot of force, though. When I'm just floating around as I am now, then no — I can't feel a thing.'

Magnolia wiped her wrist with the cloth she'd been using to grip a tighter hold on the main lever of her drinks machine and then took a sip of hot chocolate.

'Oooo, that's heavenly. Are you sure you don't want to try some? See if you can taste it?'

'Go on, then.' Patricia grasped the handle of the mug somewhat jerkily — subtle movements were harder for her to master — and brought the rim of the mug to her lips. Hot chocolate cascaded onto the floor.

'Oh no!' Magnolia exclaimed in dismay. It was going to take more than a mere cloth to clean *that* spillage up.

Patricia cackled with glee.

'I knew that was going to happen. I just wanted to do it anyway, for kicks.'

'You're like a precocious child.'

Patricia sensed Magnolia's thaw towards her was in danger of reversing. Relieving her boredom at the expense of friendship would be foolish, she realised.

'Sorry. Why don't you tell me how you became a *chocolatier*?'

And so this was how a remarkable rapport began to unfurl… as Magnolia mopped up the spilt hot chocolate and started to share with a captivated Patricia the memories of her enchanting, eye-opening summer in Bruges.

The next few days saw Magnolia and Patricia fall into an easy pattern of activity melded with growing comradery. Patricia found her anxiety at being between worlds was soothed by observing Magnolia at her craft;

Magnolia found Patricia's frank assessment of her business launch preparations valuable and refreshing.

The shop wouldn't be opening until the first week in December, but as well as experimenting with her intended product range, Magnolia had a flurry of commissions from friends-of-friends to fulfil. As such, there was an element of chocolate-making going on in the shop most days.

Magnolia usually arrived at the shop around nine-thirty in the morning — she was the first to admit that she wasn't a morning person, and on the occasions that she arrived earlier than this, she'd be irritable and lacking in concentration. She usually worked in the kitchen for around three hours, and Patricia enjoyed not knowing exactly what delicious concoctions she was going to conjure up until the exact moment she began assembling her ingredients and apparatus.

Patricia was fascinated by the tempering process and wanted to learn how to do it. Disappointingly, though, although Magnolia tried several times to teach her, it just didn't seem possible.

She couldn't feel the subtle ebb and flow of the liquid chocolate against the palette knife and increase or decrease her pressure accordingly; either the palette knife skimmed the top of the mixture aggressively and at alarming speed, splattering liquid chocolate over an impressive range of surfaces as it did so and leaving very little to work with, or it sluggishly meandered over the mixture, meaning the chocolate on top didn't cool against the marble quickly enough.

She was good at unpacking and organising supplies, though. Magnolia grew accustomed to seeing sacks of un-tempered chocolate pellets and various jars and bottles floating from delivery box to shelf under Patricia's control; on one occasion a bag split, and the ensuing cascade of hazelnuts suddenly and impressively halted in mid-air at Patricia's will. Magnolia grabbed a large bowl, and Patricia sent them safely plinking into it in twos and threes.

Lunchtimes involved a preprepared sandwich or pasta salad for Magnolia, along with a hot chocolate and a morsel of whatever sweet treat she'd been making that morning; ensconced from then on at the hot chocolate counter, Patricia would join her for a sniff of hot chocolate and a chat, which veered wildly from the inane to the meaningful.

Afternoons were generally dedicated to working on the chocolate shop's website and other marketing elements, financials, scheduling, building up a supplier network and packaging design — all done from Magnolia's laptop computer at the hot chocolate counter.

Magnolia learnt to read Patricia's moods and tailor her behaviour accordingly, particularly with regard to her chocolate making. Being open-minded and keen to share her passion, she was nevertheless conscious of and sensitive to the fact that Patricia could no longer take pleasure in the taste of chocolate — and she didn't want to taunt her with this.

She thought the best thing to do would be to completely avoid inviting Patricia's opinion on the composition and design of her chocolates. However, this actually proved to be hugely upsetting for her new friend, who wanted to be included in the artistic process and make a difference to the outcome, despite her inability to enjoy the taste of the finished result.

After a few days of Magnolia giving her the opportunity to collaborate, though, Patricia would suddenly go into a self-pitying tailspin and lament about her inability to contribute anything worthwhile. At these times, Magnolia quickly pulled back and tried to immerse herself in computer-based work instead, or encouraged Patricia to indulge in a music fest with her radio in the outbuilding, so that she could get on with the chocolate making alone.

Patricia announced one day that she could see Mark's bike shop from the front window of the chocolate shop — if she hovered a foot from the ground, tilted her head at a rather awkward angle, and extended her neck as far as possible. This proved to be a revelation for her. Mark had already popped into the chocolate shop countless times, for one random reason or another, yet it seemed Patricia's curiosity about him still hadn't been satisfied.

'His shop is called On Yer Bike,' she mused during one gawping session, head tilted at the odd forty-five-degree angle Magnolia had quickly come to recognise as her "spying on Mark" pose. 'Don't you think that sounds rather aggressive and offensive?'

Magnolia laughed. 'A lot of us said that, actually, when he first came up with it. But apparently his customers like it. They think it's playful and cheekily endearing.'

'What on earth is he doing?' Patricia suddenly exclaimed, her evaluation of the merits of the shop's name now forgotten. 'He's kissing that woman who's just walked in!' The shock made her waver in her elevated position, like a beach ball bobbing on the ocean.

'What woman?' Magnolia hurried over. 'Are you sure it's not Gavin, the mechanic? He looks a bit like Mark, from a distance.'

'No, Gavin's having far too much fun jumping on empty cardboard boxes for the recycling bin, as usual. I can just see him in the alley.'

Magnolia opened the window so that she could stretch her upper body out and therefore see more.

'That's his wife!' she admonished Patricia, shimmying backwards after a few moments. She'd been hanging so far out the window that her waist was rubbing against the windowsill. 'I can't believe you made me throw myself out the window for that!'

'Hmm?'

'That's Claire. My sister-in-law.'

'She doesn't look like a gardener.'

57

'What?'

'She looks like a supermodel. It's understandable that I'd come to the wrong conclusion.'

'I didn't say she was an actual gardener. What does a gardener look like, anyway? Oh, never mind. This is a ludicrous conversation.'

Patricia, having retreated towards the kitchen, suddenly swivelled around. Her nose twitched, and she looked at the adjoining wall, before floating back over to the open front window.

'I can smell fresh bread from the bakery!' she announced triumphantly.

'Damn, I thought my hot chocolate was special,' Magnolia joked. 'Well, I'm pleased for you. What type of bread is it today, then, do you think?'

'It's something with Italian herbs in it… oregano or thyme, maybe. That's not really Brian's style, though.' Patricia looked confused.

'His nephew owns the bakery now. He's more adventurous with his flavours.'

'Ah, that's a shame. I was hoping Brian might pop in here at some point. He was an argumentative so-and-so, you know. He had his eye on a grandfather clock I was trying to sell on. He told me I was asking far too much for it.'

'And were you?'

'Yes, but that's not the point.'

'Of course it's the point!'

'It's not the point of what I'm trying to tell you; which is that despite our differences, Brian and I rubbed along quite well. He had a good sense of humour.'

'When you had this place as your antiques shop, did you specialise in any particular area?'

'Well... we preferred furniture and avoided jewellery, but other than that, no. We certainly didn't concentrate on any one period or style.'

'What was your antique business called?' Magnolia asked, suddenly curious to know.

'Daventry's Splendid Antiques. I realise that's not funky and fresh, but such things aren't the be all and end all. Depending on the business, sometimes it's appropriate to be conservative.'

Magnolia splayed her outstretched hands in surrender. 'Hey, I'm not judging. It's not my area of expertise.'

The day drew to a close, and Magnolia gathered her belongings and located her keys ready to leave, when something suddenly dawned on her.

'What do you do when I go home?' she asked, hopping down from her stool at the hot chocolate counter and looking back at Patricia. 'It must be very boring and lonely for you here.'

Patricia shrugged. 'It was a lot worse before you came. I usually just settle down in the pantry or the outbuilding for a few hours. Obviously, I don't need sleep, but I can put myself into a certain state of suspension. Not sure how. It seems a bit like sleep, anyway. Better in a lot of ways though — I'm not disturbed by uncomfortable temperatures or bodily afflictions.'

Magnolia considered this. 'Shall I buy a little radio, instead of using my phone for music? Then you could listen to it in the evenings. That weird seventies stuff that you like. You'd have to keep the volume setting really low, though.'

Patricia brightened. 'Ooo, yes please!'

And so it came to be, that anyone happening to walk past the chocolate shop between six and ten in the evenings, if they were particularly keen of hearing and extremely nosy, would hear a joyful, not-completely bad voice singing along to theatrical rock whist a sweeping brush bobbed around the kitchen of its own accord.

Chapter Eight

Much as the shop was becoming Magnolia's sanctuary, as well as her fledgling business, from time to time she felt the need to physically distance herself in order to look at things from a fresh perspective. Sourcing stoneware mugs for her desired hot chocolate counter was the ideal opportunity to do so. Hence it was, that on a hot, gleaming day — one of those rare days when the world seemed to be melting away, whether it be roads, foliage, or five-bar gates — Magnolia found herself driving towards her best friends' farm.

From Magnolia's market town home at the foot of the North Yorkshire moors, it was only a delightful three-mile journey until immersion in deep countryside. A journey she didn't make often enough, she considered, as she drove the winding country lanes to Beth and Dan's Dexter beef farm in a charming and verdant crease of land to the west.

She'd met them both at college; they'd all started out studying business, but whilst Magnolia and Beth went on to do a business degree, Dan embraced agricultural business management instead. Beth and Dan were married not long after university, and several years later, they had a small yet successful herd; their grass-fed Dexter beef was widely sought after, and their combined business acumen ensured they made a healthy living.

They had a four-year-old son, Dominic, and feeling the desire to do something else besides parenting and helping with the business side of the farm, Beth had recently established her own handmade pottery business. Magnolia had already decided that she'd use her friend's quirky stoneware mugs on her hot chocolate counter, but she wanted to visit the farm that day to see Beth actually ensconced in her workshop, to see what delightful offerings she had in mind.

It had been a year since she'd last visited the farm — between the three of them, they usually chose to catch up every two or three weeks in an idiosyncratic pub in a village halfway between their homes — so it was inevitable that she would take a wrong turn at some point; her poor sense of direction was embarrassing. Refusing to succumb to panic, she determined she'd find her way eventually, and having finally glimpsed the tell-tale Dexter cows in their green idyll — they were much smaller than most other cows around here — she allowed her mind to drift a little to memories of the barbecue last year.

It had been the ideal opportunity for Dan and Beth to show off their award-winning Dexter beef to a crowd of close to a hundred people. They'd served short ribs in a lip-smacking, spiced sauce as well as steaks and burgers with herby garlic butter and tomato mayonnaise. Magnolia, as a pescetarian, was overwhelmed to discover they'd also prepared whole sea bass and sardines alongside char-grilled squid — all sizzling in a heady combination of lemon, garlic, chilli, basil and thyme marinade. Her stomach now rumbled at the thought.

'Well, that was a rollercoaster ride!' she exclaimed, arriving at her friends' farm in a cloud of dust.

'Yeah, I definitely need to fill in the track and smooth it out a bit,' Dan said ruefully. He hitched the hay net on his shoulder to a more comfortable position and looked on as his black Labrador, Carlos, approached Magnolia joyfully for a bit of a stroke. 'Having said that, I think it's better if you don't drive down it so fast.'

Magnolia winced. 'Yeah, I'll remember that.'

Dan laughed and slapped her affectionately on the shoulder. 'Come on, I'll take you to Beth's workshop.'

They walked companionably alongside each other, passing a huge barn, which was almost empty, except for a twenty-something skinny guy in green overalls, who was throwing courgettes, with great concentration and panache, into barrels spaced at varying distances from where he stood. Magnolia noticed that his position was marked with a huge cross chalked on the floor, and each barrel stood in its own chalk circle identifying its particular distance away.

'That's Harrington,' Dan declared as they walked on, as if this was all the explanation necessary.

Magnolia was curious to know more, but he changed the subject.

'So how's Chocolate World going? Are you bored of faffing about with melting and swirling all that chocolate yet?'

'It's going fine. No, I'm not bored — I'm enjoying it. There's more stuff to think about with the shop than I realised at first, but everything's fine. How's the Fun Farm going? Are you bored of faffing about with moving cows from one field to another yet?'

Dan gave a great booming laugh like Father Christmas, and a startled chicken zoomed across their path in a flurry of feathers and sharp squawks. 'I suppose I deserve that,' he said, stopping at the heavy oak door of Beth's barn-conversion workshop and rapping his huge knuckles on it briskly before throwing it wide open.

'Nolly's here!' he announced.

'Don't let Carlos in!' Beth shrieked from within, rising from a butcher's block table strewn with odd pieces of half-finished pottery. She wiped her hands on her star-spangled dungarees, threw herself towards Magnolia, and drew her into a warm hug, her ash-blonde hair almost falling out of the messy high ponytail she'd shoved it into. Dan faded into the background, with Carlos lolloping obediently at his heels.

Beth drew back appraisingly. 'You look all bright-eyed — as though you've finally found something to fire you up.'

Magnolia shrugged her shoulders happily. 'I suppose I have.'

'Sit down, then and tell me all about it. Tea?'

'Yes, please.' Magnolia looked around, wondering where to sit.

'Do you want a wonky willow mug?' Beth asked, holding aloft one of her wonderfully unusual creations. 'I mean to drink out of now, not to take away. Actually, you can take it away with you as well, if you like. I know how obsessed you are with trees. The shape of the mug is meant to be wonky, by the way. It's organic. Free from the shackles of expectation.'

'Ooo, if only we could all be "free from the shackles of expectation".'

'It's one of the few things I'm getting gloriously better at.' Beth grinned and playfully threw teabags into the mugs from a two-foot distance. 'And throwing tea bags into mugs, of course. I suppose you haven't been in here for a couple of years,' she continued, filling the kettle at a clean yet paint-spotted Belfast sink. 'That side is the chaos zone, that side is the calm zone.' She gesticulated left then right like an air traffic controller.

Her pottery wheel was in the chaos zone, along with a huge ramshackle dresser with numerous doors and drawers, most falling off their hinges and runners to reveal the varied materials of her trade, in no particular order, alarmingly close to spilling out. A plethora of tools, like surgical torture instruments, littered a clay-splattered table, and various sacks and receptacles teetered in stacks against the walls.

The calm zone was almost entirely dedicated to a trestle table, neatly positioned against the wall, with three shelves above it; a cornucopia of Beth's finished wares were displayed here, as if in a proper shop, showcasing her offbeat yet obvious talent.

The butcher's block table that Beth had risen from on Magnolia's arrival was in the centre of the workshop, and it was here that Beth motioned for them to sit.

'So, how's it all going, being self-employed?'

As the kettle boiled, Magnolia filled her friend in on progress with her new business venture so far, as well as her plans leading up to the opening and beyond.

'I'm nowhere near your stage yet, though.' Magnolia looked around the workshop admiringly. 'You seem really sorted. The only money I'm making at the moment is from the sporadic commissions I get for weddings and corporate events. It means I'm still able to treat myself to a bottle of *Pouilly Fumé* at the weekend, but whether I can make a long-term living out of running my own business is yet to be seen.'

'It's not for everyone,' Beth admitted. 'I've fallen asleep in here several times whilst trying to finish off "just one more job". Only last month I was hand painting a fiddly tea set around midnight and I just dropped off. I woke up at about three o' clock in the morning with my elbow all wet from knocking over a glass of water, and a fuchsia handprint on my cheek from the paint I was using. And my neck was in spasm. And you really don't want to know what state the house is in — it's far messier than in here.

'Having said that, I'm able to drop Dominic off at pre-school and collect him every day. We usually go down to the stream for a paddle as well, and to look for interesting creatures when the weather's good like it is now. Plus, every now and then I have a pie-making frenzy; steak and ale, chicken and mushroom… *salmon en croute*, if I'm feeling fancy. I shove them all in the freezer and we live off them for weeks when I'm busy in here. It stops Dan falling off his tractor from lack of calories, anyway. Talking of calories, didn't you bring any chocolates?'

Magnolia rolled her eyes. 'You asked me not to! You said you were on a diet.'

'Well, since then, I've come to terms with the fact I'm never going to be slim.'

'You're an enviable shape. You look amazing in those vintage fifties dresses you wear for special occasions.'

Beth's eyes brightened. 'I've bought a new one! Red and white polka dots with a massive petticoat.'

She suddenly jumped up from the table, tea remembered. 'Oh, you'll never guess what Dominic said the other day!' She looked over her shoulder at Magnolia with a wide grin, before finally finishing the refreshments process. She handed a mug to Magnolia and sat back down at the table, shaking her fringe, which always seemed to need cutting, out of her eyes.

'He's hardly ever allowed in here — only when my guilt over being a crap mother kicks in — but he's seen me working clay on the wheel from scratch quite a few times. Anyway, he genuinely thought it was cow muck! He thought everything I make is from cow shit that Dan shovels up and brings to me in the workshop, all fresh and warm and ready to turn into mugs and plates.'

'Now that would be an impressive self-sufficiency enterprise.'

'Absolutely!' Beth tilted her head, considering something. 'Actually, there will be some small percentage of cow shit in the clay, won't there? It's a natural product dug out of the ground, after all. My son is a genius. Oh, but that's nothing compared to the baked bean. Did I tell you about the baked bean?'

'Huh? No.' Magnolia looked at Beth in amused bewilderment; catch-ups with her old college friend were always delightfully yet exhaustingly animated, veering sharply from one topic of conversation to another.

'Dominic, the little rascal; he put a baked bean in the corner of his bedroom windowsill that he'd squirreled away from his lunch one day. He was testing my cleaning standards. You know, seeing how long it would take me to discover it.'

'And? How long?'

'Well… you can't really rely on a four-year-old's concept of time, but it must have been nearly three months. He said he put it there when Nana Grace came to visit, which was the second May bank holiday weekend. I found it just a couple of weeks ago. He'd forgotten about it, by then. It was all black and furry.'

'That's gross!' Magnolia wrinkled her nose.

'It was right in the corner! I'd have seen it earlier, otherwise. I cleaned the windowsills before then — just in a slapdash way.'

'I don't know why you tell me these stories and then spend twice as long afterwards defending your reputation,' Magnolia laughed. 'I meant the bean was gross, not that your cleaning standards were. But just so that you know — I'm never letting you anywhere near my chocolate-making kitchen.'

'*Touché.*'

'Here you go.' Magnolia drew a small box from her bag. 'Dark chocolate coated ginger. I knew you'd change your mind. And they're not as calorific as most of my other chocolates.'

Beth stood from her chair, reached forward and grabbed Magnolia's shoulders exuberantly, planting a kiss on the top of her head. 'You're an absolute angel.' She sat back down, opened the box and popped a piece of chocolate ginger in her mouth.

'Hey, do you remember at college, when I was really upset over Aaron Baxter dumping me, and you gave me one of your super-duper expensive chocolates to cheer me up?'

'Yeah, of course — those chocolates were way better than Aaron Baxter.' They both giggled.

'It was an espresso martini truffle. It tasted amazing, but I was so worried that our business studies teacher would detect alcohol on my breath!'

Magnolia laughed. 'We were so goody-two-shoes initially, weren't we? Getting all worried about liqueur chocolates. Then, by the second term we were drinking vodka in the toilets at break times.'

'Not every break time! Christ, don't be repeating that in front of Dan.'

'Only every now and then, actually... but I can hardly believe we did it at all, now.'

Suddenly there was an almighty thump from above.

'What on earth was that?' Magnolia splashed tea on her wrist as she looked to the ceiling.

Beth waved her hand dismissively. 'Oh, don't worry, it'll just be Harrington. A tile fell off the roof a couple of nights ago. He'll just be fixing it.'

Beth laughed.

A man of many talents, it seems. 'Dan and I walked past him on the way over here. He was chucking courgettes into barrels. What was that all about?'

'Oh, he'll have been making a video for his YouTube followers. He's always doing random weird shit like that. He's quite popular on there.'

70

Magnolia raised her eyebrows. 'I hope his camera didn't catch me walking past gormlessly in the background.'

'I'm sure you'd be a delightful addition! Anyway,' Beth drummed her fingers on the table, 'I feel like I've being terribly narcissistic. I haven't stopped talking about my own life. Tell me more about your chocolate shop.'

'There's nothing else to tell you yet, really. I sent you all the drawings showing how it'll look once all the fixtures and fittings are in. Until I get closer to opening, I'm just using the place to make the chocolates for the special requests I get for parties and weddings... and practising with recipes and product lines.'

And chatting to a ghost called Patricia all day, but let's not go down that path.

'Well, let's talk about your hot chocolate mugs, then.' Beth jumped up excitedly. 'This is the style I thought you might like,' she said, retrieving three hand thrown pottery mugs from a side bench. 'They're stoneware clay, and I can do pretty much any glaze you like, but I thought these three colours were the best: burnt orange, emerald green and cobalt blue.'

'They're marvellous!' Magnolia enthused, reaching for the burnt orange one and rolling it in her palms. 'I love the way the glaze changes to a darker tone towards the bottom. And the bulbous shape is perfect. Do you think you could make the handle really ornate and curvaceous? And put little feet on the base?'

71

'You mean like the feet on a trivet? Quite stumpy?'

'Exactly! See, I knew you'd understand what I wanted.'

Beth shrugged nonchalantly. 'Absolutely... how many do you want?'

'Twenty would be good to start with. Would that be OK? And then could I ask for more at a later date, if I need them? I'm not having a café, just a hot chocolate counter. I thought it would complement the shop and elevate the customer experience — you know, allow people to linger and immerse their senses fully.'

'Twenty's fine. Your vision sounds great.' Beth slurped her tea. 'I can't wait to see it. You won't be able to get rid of me.'

Magnolia grinned. 'What do you think of these?' she asked, plucking four slices of agate rock from her bag; each one a breathtaking burst of colour, like an exploding galaxy in the palm of her hand. 'They're so smooth and thin — I thought they'd be ideal as coasters for the mugs.'

'They're gorgeous, and they'd match well, but don't you think people might pinch them?'

'Hmm, maybe... I'll have a think about it.'

After a couple of hours with Beth, Magnolia departed; taking with her half a dozen delightful duck eggs, fresh from the coop, that she intended to make a red onion frittata with, as well as a buzz of energy from having broken out into different surroundings, chatting with her friend, and sharing creative ideas. She felt carefree and light-hearted too; being with Beth always reminded her of their shared college days.

Later, frittata successfully made and devoured, with a burst of new ideas plumping up the notebook beside her as she sat on the sofa with her legs tucked under herself like a cat, Magnolia's thoughts drifted back in time.

College, sixteen years previously…

Magnolia hated having to wake up at six-thirty, hated the bus journey into town, and hated the inevitability that she'd wear completely the wrong clothes for any given day's weather. She'd lost count of the times she'd had to carry her snuggly coat, scarf trailing in her wake, college folders slipping from her grip, on the days that the sun decided it was going to smash through after all. Then there were the times she'd be shivering in a light cotton dress and open-toed sandals when the teasing sun decided, despite a promising start, that it couldn't be bothered, leaving gun-metal grey to reign supreme.

The only comfort that carried her through these first weeks of college life was the anticipation of a tiny bag of chocolate truffles.

She'd alight from the bus two stops earlier than the college, her destination a charming little independent chocolate shop tucked away from the main thoroughfare.

The first three times she visited, her request for a few truffles from the "choose your own" counter — where the premium, fresh truffles were displayed — was met with the same response; the woman serving her tried very hard not to be condescending.

It was suggested that perhaps Magnolia would like to choose one of the chunky bars of chocolate on the shelves instead of these more expensive chocolates. Then, the gentle warning that she'd only get five or six of these finer chocolates for the same price as "the basic" chocolate. Magnolia didn't mind so much — she conceded it was unusual for a sixteen-year-old to prize premium chocolate above anything else her limited pocket money could buy. Before long though, the owner Josie, came to recognise her and anticipate her tastes.

She'd select five or six truffles on each occasion; always one milk chocolate champagne truffle — so decadent! — often one key lime cheesecake truffle, which had a delightful zing of powdered lime zest sprinkled on top of the white chocolate shell — and the remainder dependent on her mood.

Magnolia and Beth became friends in the fifth week of term. Beth's look back then was *Moulin Rouge*-chic meets farmyard scruffy. She favoured flamboyantly patterned thigh-length silk kimonos and velvet ballerina flats, mismatched with men's jeans and her hair loose and extravagantly tousled. Magnolia thought she was wonderfully intriguing, but she didn't dare attempt to start a conversation with her.

Beth had met Aaron a few weeks previously, in the summer holidays, on a — by all accounts — glamorous trip to Vienna that the orchestra they were both members of had organised; Beth played the viola, Aaron the violin. Instantly attracted to one another, they quickly became a couple, and were ecstatic to realise that they'd both be attending the same local college in the autumn. That is, until Aaron decided he wanted to chase the same girl as many other male members of the business studies class; an Icelandic beauty called Helda, with glossy white-blonde hair, an immaculate complexion and a seemingly flawless figure; plus, absolutely no interest whatsoever in any of the guys buzzing around her.

The class was halfway through a role play exercise on job interviews one morning, the tutor having just called a ten-minute break, when Aaron told Beth he was dumping her. Understandably, Beth had been very upset, ran immediately from the room, and when Magnolia went out after her, declared that she didn't want to attend the second part of the role play exercise, as Aaron was a member of her group, the class having been split into five teams.

Magnolia comforted her, said she shouldn't let such a knob-head ruin her chances of getting a good grade, and offered to switch teams with her so she wouldn't have to be in close proximity to him. Beth gratefully accepted this suggestion, they had a restorative coffee together and the now legendary espresso martini truffle

— one each — and Magnolia, so far in these first few weeks of college having only had pleasant yet fleeting interactions with her fellow students, found herself making a firm and lasting friend.

As heady teenage crushes and flirtations unravelled in varying degrees from something to nothing, some more embarrassing in hindsight than others; as new friendships forged over consumption of cheap alcohol, cigarettes and the music and social movements of the moment either flourished or fizzled out; as a hundred college reports were written and a hundred plates of tacos and burgers delivered from kitchen to restaurant table in temporary, casual jobs; amidst the carousel of study hard, play hard, work hard, find your identity; Magnolia's love for good chocolate endured.

Chapter Nine

Although it was a pleasant summer, Magnolia and Patricia hadn't sat outside together on the strip of grass behind the shop kitchen before. This was because Magnolia's time at the shop had so far only been within a haze of productivity, but also because they'd realised that Patricia became almost invisible to Magnolia's eye in the bright sunlight, making it difficult to carry a conversation. Not to mention the fact that they'd had no desire to have a conversation with each other until recently.

But now, here they were. Two tradesmen were currently installing Magnolia's new shelf brackets, and she wanted to be close by, but not too close. Ostensibly reading, she sat on a picnic chair with a book on her lap, whilst Patricia sat in a slice of shadow by the outbuilding, legs outstretched.

Fortuitously, a friend of Mark's was in the process of converting an old water tower into a home, and between the two of them — over a night out where the *mojitos* were flowing generously — they'd persuaded him to give Magnolia a small proportion of the original copper water pipes for her shop. In exchange, however, they both somehow promised to help with the interior painting and decorating of the water tower. For months to come, whenever Magnolia saw the colour oxblood, she'd be reminded of the deep ache in her shoulders as a result of painting the endless and gargantuan old water tower walls.

The copper pipes were worth it, though.

Magnolia looked around at her outdoor space. It was small, but given that she'd be spending a lot of time here going forward, she decided she'd ask Claire if she could magic up some potted trees and maybe a clutch of wisteria to wander over the contours of the outbuilding. Just how long did wisteria take to establish itself? Would she have the delightfully winding and drooping fluffy blooms by next year, or did it take longer than that? It'd be great if she could have a little slice of nature right at her fingertips, for when she wanted to escape the shop but didn't have time to go far.

Patricia sniffed the air luxuriantly. 'The wind's certainly blowing in the right direction today. Jed's bread smells fantastic.'

'Mmm, it does. What do you think he's baking at the moment?'

'Bubbling cheddar and balsamic onion,' Patricia said confidently.

That's what it was actually called. He liked using adjectives in the names of his bread.

Magnolia thought it was a shame Patricia and Jed couldn't meet each other. She wanted to entice him into the shop at some point so that Patricia could at least see what he was like, but this was difficult to achieve without seeming too pushy, and even more so with Jed being gone from his bakery by two o' clock most days anyway, having started his bread-making before dawn.

'Something I'm curious about,' Patricia went on, as she ruffled the grass — she did this by means of intense eye contact, rather than by hand, 'if your time in Bruges was twelve years ago, how is it that you're only just opening your own chocolate shop now?'

'I came back to reality with a bit of a bump.' Magnolia looked pained at the memory. 'I was a bit naïve.'

She told Patricia about her first chocolate-making adventure on coming back to England.

Autumn Food Festival, twelve years previously…

After Bruges, despite needing to concentrate on her final year university studies, Magnolia was keen to continue the momentum of her chocolate-making. Whilst she had plans to make chocolate Christmas gifts for her family and friends later in the year, she also wanted to embrace the craft in a commercial sense; to start trying to make a real living as a *chocolatier* as soon as possible.

She therefore found herself signing up as a trader at a local market town's annual autumn food festival. With over a hundred stalls, from artisan smokeries to niche distilleries taking a space, they were expecting thousands of visitors over the festival weekend.

Tempted to showcase a vast array of delights, Magnolia somehow reined in her enthusiasm and, with economies of scale in mind, sensibly decided to focus on just four different products: spiced pumpkin truffles, shaped and decorated to resemble actual pumpkins; hazelnut truffles; solid bars of dark chocolate with dried cherry and crumbled amaretti biscuit; and solid bars of milk chocolate with cinnamon, nutmeg and ginger. Keen to use flavours representative of the season, she nevertheless worried that she wasn't appealing to a wide enough range of palates.

The weather on the Saturday of the food festival was listless and mizzly. Dread now curdling with fatigue in her stomach as she threw back the curtains — she'd been making truffles until well past midnight, two nights running — Magnolia set about dosing herself with fresh coffee and tried to recapture her previous optimism.

Two hours later, safely ensconced in her designated marquee, her relief at having set up her stall before the lazy rain gathered force was short-lived. Her produce had been protected from the elements, but that wasn't much good if her potential customers were deterred from making the journey to see what she had to offer.

Peering anxiously out of the plastic window of the marquee, she saw that the field they were pitched on was fast becoming a quagmire outside. Only a few grim-faced patrons battled onwards, their young children rushing ahead to gleefully splosh about in the abundant puddles.

Those who did make it into the marquee were immediately attracted to the coffee bar. Unfortunately for Magnolia, they then invariably bee-lined for an artisan pie and pasty stall, which offered hot apple and cinnamon and banana and caramel varieties as well as the savouries. With such a comforting option available, chocolates just weren't on most people's wish list as an immediate treat, and she only benefited from the custom of those seeking to buy gifts or something to enjoy later.

One hour passed, two hours passed, and her customers were few and far between.

It suddenly dawned on her that making truffles with fresh cream for her first commercial event was a terrible mistake. It wouldn't have been quite so bad if they'd been made with alcohol, which preserved them for longer, but as it was, she now had just a few days before they'd need to be eaten or binned.

Then, a sudden gust of wind blew a corner flap of the marquee roof back, just above Magnolia's carefully constructed display, which included vintage cake stands for the chocolates, to give varying height, as well as ornate photo frames housing her product descriptions written in painstaking calligraphy on premium card. The canvas above settled into a new position, promptly creating a small yet steady thoroughfare for the rain to do what gravity intended — stream over a good half of Magnolia's table.

Panicked, she hastily set about rearranging everything, but not before some of the cardboard packaging boxes caught the tell-tale blooms of fat water droplets, with one droplet even finding its way behind the glass of a photo frame — destroying the text completely.

She'd had enough. When a beaming seven or eight-year-old boy dragged his mother over moments later, attracted by the pumpkin truffles, she virtually gave away half her stock to him. He couldn't believe his luck, cheeks apple-red with the cold popping even more prominently as his smile deepened, whilst his mother looked at her with confusion falling into a curious mix of sympathy and gratitude.

Not long after, she packed up and left.

She'd have made a modest profit if all her produce had sold, but with the cost of ingredients and packaging, along with the cost of the stall, having only sold about a third of her produce, she was probably down by around two hundred pounds — and that didn't even factor in her time and effort. Bruges had certainly been a more captive audience.

But at least she'd made someone happy.

'So — that quashed my enthusiasm for a while,' Magnolia concluded with a sigh.

'I can see how it would,' Patricia sympathised.

Max, one of the tradesmen, appeared in the kitchen doorway; in his mid-thirties, Magnolia guessed, he had the face of someone much younger, and seemed to be constantly smiling. He had calves like the brass bellows you'd find by the open fireplace in an old-fashioned country inn, and the dense and profuse tattoos on his arms rippled along with his biceps in such a way that you couldn't actually make out their definition.

'The piping brackets for your shelves aren't going to match, you know,' he declared.

'What do you mean?'

'It won't be uniform. The left wall won't look the same as the right wall.'

'I know. That's how I want it to be. I want it to look neat, but quite random. And as many right angles as possible — well, you know what I mean. I don't want the piping to go directly from one point to another. Aesthetically, it'll look more intriguing.'

'Ah, OK. Good. I get it.'

His smile grew wider than normal and he tilted his head to one side. 'Does that fancy-pants drinks machine of yours make iced coffee as well? It's so hot in there that I think my tattoos are in danger of melting off.'

'No, it doesn't. But maybe the owner can find some ice in her fridge freezer and knock something together for you,' Magnolia said kindly, rising from her chair.

'Youngsters today — no stamina,' Patricia contributed, inevitably to be ignored.

In the kitchen, Magnolia retrieved a couple of ice cube trays from the small freezer whilst Max looked on. 'Does your mate want iced coffee as well?' she asked him.

'Yes, please. How are you going to crush the ice cubes though?'

'You want the ice cubes to be crushed?' Magnolia gave a short, surprised laugh. 'Well... I don't have a blender here, but I suppose I can fold the ice cubes in a tea towel and bash them with a rolling pin.'

He grinned. 'Great.'

As she set about doing so, Patricia wandered in.

'Hey, maybe you can get your ghost to stamp on them with her feet instead. That'll crush them,' Max joked, with impeccable yet unconscious timing. 'You won't believe the stories I've heard about this place.'

'Oh, please let me give him something *really* worth talking about?' Patricia implored Magnolia, sidling over. 'In a heartbeat, I could make him completely unconcerned about whether his ice is cubed or crushed.'

'Absolutely not,' Magnolia snapped.

'I was only joking,' Max replied.

Shit. Well, at least it's interesting to see that his smile isn't a permanent fixture after all.

He looked quite hurt, though.

'Sorry, I thought you asked for a shot of whisky in the coffee too,' Magnolia improvised, as a blush crept up her neck and snatched at her cheeks. 'I don't think

84

that's a good idea, seeing as you're fitting shelves and using hammers and saws and suchlike.'

'What?'

Arrghh, I've just made the whole thing ridiculously worse. Why over-elaborate with a lie? I should have just pretended I was affronted by his suggestion of a ghost.

He definitely looked offended.

'I was only joking too!' she said brightly.

Now he looked alarmed.

'Sorry… I think the heat is going to my head,' she continued.

His smile finally reappeared This, he could understand.

To minimise the chances of saying the wrong thing again, Magnolia finished preparing the drinks as quickly as possible, before making a hasty retreat back outside.

'That was fun!' Patricia chortled, having shadowed her along the way. 'What's next?' Magnolia shook her head and pinched the point between her eyes in weary mortification.

For ten minutes they sat in their own little cocoon, enjoying the sunshine, and on Magnolia's part, recuperating from embarrassment. Then Magnolia turned to Patricia quizzically. 'What do you miss most from before?'

Patricia smiled in beatific contemplation. 'Lobster macaroni cheese; that sweet, succulent meat and unctuous, oozing Gruyere sauce enhanced with butter and wine... and feeling sun-warmed blades of grass tickling my skin — I can't feel them now, you know.

'Also, I miss wandering around the moors; all those spectacular views and the fresh air. My son used to accompany me on walks sometimes. He preferred the dense woodland, but I definitely preferred the moorland. Especially in late summer; that's when the heather comes out and bathes the ground purple for miles around. I love that colour.'

I knew that the moment I met you, Magnolia thought, with a secret smile of amused affection. *It's plain to see from your choice of clothes and makeup.*

'And even in my later years, I wasn't afraid of tricky footing and a bit of an incline,' Patricia continued. 'It was all part of the adventure. I can see some of the moorland if I sit on the outbuilding roof, you know. Sometimes it's cruelly mocking — a reminder of what I've lost. But mostly it's consoling. Of course, I also miss...'

She stopped abruptly, her facial expression becoming a mask. 'I don't want to talk about myself,' she continued firmly. 'Can you tell me more about your adventures instead? I've been confined to this shop for God knows how long, with nothing to stimulate me, just wallowing in my own thoughts and regrets, and I could really do with hearing someone else's fresh and fabulous life story.'

'Of course — I understand.' A ladybird landed on the back of Magnolia's hand, and she gently transferred it to the grass behind her. 'I'll tell you more about my journey here, but it really isn't fabulous.'

Patricia couldn't have looked more like she was settling in to watch a blockbuster movie if she'd had a box of popcorn on her lap.

'So — the autumn food festival wasn't the only time that I battled with the weather,' Magnolia continued. 'I built up my confidence and experience a bit over the next few years, with special commissions for contacts of family and friends. But then I had a nightmare trying to stop the sun destroying a huge cake I'd decorated with lashings of chocolate for my dad's sixtieth birthday party. It wouldn't have been so bad, but my mum talked the cake up to the guests beforehand as though it was going to be something spectacular.'

'Ooo, tell me about that.'

Mallorca, seven years previously…

'Oh, Mum! You need to keep the blinds down and the air conditioning on in here otherwise the chocolate will just roll off the cake.'

Magnolia stood in the doorway of the kitchen at her parent's Mallorcan retirement villa and noted with exasperation the beams of blazing sunlight striking the worktops from every angle.

'But it seems such a shame to block the sun out,' Lauren Aitken responded, opening an overhead cupboard to check her gin and tonic supplies. 'Your

87

father and I have lived with the miserable British weather for far too long. We deserve some sunshine in the last days of our lives.'

'I'm sure you can cope with a cool kitchen for two or three hours.' Magnolia systematically snapped shut the blinds and flipped the air conditioning on. 'Have you cleared a space in the fridge?'

'Um.'

Magnolia opened the fridge door, 'Evidently not.'

'You can't take those out!'

'Mum, you don't need twenty litres of bottled water in there. Quite frankly, I'm freaking out. Creating a forty-centimetre-high cake and decorating it with chocolate to look like the *Sa Calobra*, whilst we're experiencing a thirty-five-degree heat wave, is a big undertaking.'

'Okay, fair enough.' Lauren shrugged her shoulders and flicked her sunglasses from the top of her head back to her face. 'I'll leave you to it. I made five sponge cakes instead of three, so you've got extra in case something goes wrong. They're in the corner cupboard. I'll be by the pool if you need me. Remember, your dad's due back from his golf at seven, so…'

'So, I need to magically replicate one of the most famous cycling climbs in Europe out of cake and chocolate and leave no trace of doing so by the time he's back. Yep, I've got it.'

As her mother sashayed out of the kitchen, Magnolia fleetingly wondered whether necking a couple of shots of gin would help her nerves; then made do with the comforting thought that this time tomorrow it would all be over.

The next day, Magnolia and Claire were sitting in the shade on the terrace, shelling fresh almonds that they'd just picked from the trees in the villa garden. Magnolia had done all she could to layer and sculpt the cake with chocolate, and was now trying to block the experience from her memory.

Lauren was in front of them, swimming laps in the pool and then sunbathing on a lounger intermittently — some complicated "exercise-rest" programme that Magnolia hadn't yet figured out the rules of. She'd prepared most of the food for the birthday dinner party that morning, having chosen recipes that Joe liked, that were representative of Mallorca, were impressive, but most importantly, with a bit of forethought, didn't require a lot of manic buzzing around the kitchen in the hour or so before the event.

'Tell me again why Damian didn't come out here with you?' Claire enquired.

Magnolia screwed up her face. 'Because we don't like each other enough to spend a whole week in each other's company.'

Claire shook her head in mock despair.

'I don't even like it when he stays overnight. He's a morning person, but I'm an evening person. He's up and in the kitchen, bashing pots and pans around like a buffalo and wittering on about inane things that he wants me to give an opinion on, whilst I'm still in a sleep fog. Then he likes to go to bed really early and I have to turn the TV volume down low and tiptoe around like a fairy. He doesn't even leave a bedside light on for me, so when I do eventually go to bed it takes me half an hour to find my way there in the dark.'

'I'm surprised you manage to have any sex.'

'Well, somehow, we do. Though whether it's worth putting up with all the other stuff for... let's just say that the scales of balance are beginning to tip the other way.'

'Aren't you missing him at all? Since you've been out here?'

Magnolia shrugged. 'No. Not even a little bit. I suppose that says it all, doesn't it?'

Claire did the funny eyebrow wiggle she often did unconsciously, which basically meant: *I see your reasoning, I love you for who you are, but I'm worried about where you're generally going in life.*

'Let's change the subject,' Magnolia implored, taking a gulp of water from a tall, condensation-dripping glass by her elbow.

'OK. Do you think you'd like to live here?' Claire asked. She threw a particularly plump almond into the bowl, then changed her mind and popped it into her mouth instead.

'Nah,' Magnolia responded without hesitation. 'It's great for a holiday, but the landscape isn't green enough. It's too craggy. And I'd get sick of it being hot all the time. Would you like to live here?'

Claire shook her head. 'No, for the same reasons as you said. Plus, we want to have children, and I'd like them to be brought up in the UK. I think Mark would quite like to live here, though. Francisco — your dad's friend who owns the bike shop in the town — has been filling his head with ideas about having a bike rental section of the business. I guess it could be lucrative in North Yorkshire, but even more so here.'

'But there are more suppliers competing for the demand here.'

'True. There've been a few hints though that Francisco wants to retire soon and wants to partner with someone who'll eventually take over his shop.'

'Do you think Mark would seriously be interested in that?'

'I think it's just pie in the sky... but you never know.'

At that moment, Mark and Joe returned from their gruelling bike ride up to the lighthouse, noisily professing how knackered and in need of a beer they were, and the conversation morphed into talk of preparations for the party that night.

As beer caps popped from bottles, Magnolia guessed how it was going to pan out with Claire and Mark: they'd stay in the UK, and Claire would pretty much let Mark do whatever he wanted with his existing shop, whether that was rentals or something else, as long as it didn't interfere with their upcoming wedding and baby plans.

Joe Aitken's sixtieth birthday celebration was a sophisticated *al fresco soirée* on the terrace of the villa, attended by more than thirty family members and friends. There were exactly sixty candles artfully arranged around the terrace providing an enchanting ambiance, whilst the fragrance of fresh basil, thyme and mint from abundant clay pots mingled beautifully with the heady cooking aromas.

Lauren had made an impressive feast; *caldereta de langosta,* a lobster stew, gloriously flavoured with garlic and tomatoes, as well as a trio of baked salt cod, which proved pleasingly theatrical when the crust was cracked to reveal the succulent, delicate fish beneath. This was accompanied by *trempó*, a fresh salad glistening with extra virgin olive oil, *samfaina*, a baked aubergine and pepper dish, and saffron rice.

The wine was flowing at just the right rate, the music was the perfect tempo, and there seemed to be some pre-arranged dress code of chiffon and linen.

In the picture-perfect surroundings, Magnolia thought the cake looked particularly jarring. An ornate pedestal table from the lounge — which Lauren usually used for elaborate fresh flower displays — had been positioned just behind the primary dining table, thankfully a little further away from the trestle tables most of the guests were seated at, and the cake loomed from the extended height provided.

Joe gave a heartfelt and witty speech, expressing gratitude for his family and friends, and demonstrating delight at his ability to wake each morning with a great adventure in mind for the day ahead. He enthused rather too much about his daughter's talent in transforming the cakes his wife had made into a magical showpiece, and ignored Magnolia's pained facial expressions imploring him to cease.

'Right then, let's conquer this magnificent mountain!' he finally declared, brandishing the cake knife jubilantly.

'It looks like an ant hill,' Magnolia whispered despairingly to Claire, who was sat next to her. 'Or a giant cow pat.'

Claire giggled, squeezing her hand consolingly. 'No, it doesn't. You can clearly see the little chocolate cyclists. Why would there be half a dozen cyclists pedalling their way up a giant cow pat?'

They both collapsed into fits of giggles.

As knife met cake and the whole thing collapsed ungracefully, there were whoops and cheers from everyone present; except Magnolia, who bit her lip and cringed. Actually, she considered, it looked better now. Insofar as all cakes, whether impressive or inferior, looked similarly decimated once the cake knife plunged forth.

In the airport coffee shop on the way home, though, Magnolia was struck by renewed embarrassment as she scrolled through photos of the party with Claire. 'Christ Almighty, I wish Mum had asked for a golf-themed cake instead,' she said, grimacing at the *Sa Calobra* cake on its pedestal in the background. She couldn't even bring herself to look at the photos where the cake was the prime focus. 'I'm sure Dad prefers golf to cycling. A lovely, flat golf course would have been far easier to replicate than a humongous mountain. The chocolate kept sliding off the damn thing. What a disaster.'

'Your dad loved it!' Claire insisted. 'And everyone else did too. They were amazed that you'd managed to do it, given the crazy conditions.'

'Well, it's put me off chocolate making totally.'

'No way.' A cheeky, self-satisfied smile crept across Claire's face. 'I want you to make chocolate truffles for our wedding — loads of them. Just dinky little truffles, not humongous cake mountains. You'll do it, won't you? I'll be upset beyond belief if you don't.'

'Yeah, I guess I can manage truffles without having a meltdown,' Magnolia conceded, a smile gradually emerging. 'Especially if it's for your wedding — you've definitely got me with that one.'

A harassed Mark appeared with a tray of hot drinks and toasted sandwiches. 'I completely forgot what you both wanted — it was chaos city up there and I just had to grab whatever jumped out at me,' he declared. Claire whipped her phone off the table just in time, before the tray clattered down in its place. 'I have three different types of coffee, and I haven't got a clue what's in your sandwiches. I just asked for "veggie" about five times, and this is what I was given. They better have made mine a bacon sandwich, though.' He slumped into his chair as though thoroughly depleted.

'You're my hero. It's as if you're a lion who's had to scour the African plains to find sustenance for your lioness, whatever the cost,' Claire quipped.

'That would have been easier,' Mark grumbled. Then he took a bite of his bacon sandwich and cheered up somewhat. Magnolia and Claire simultaneously peered under the top of their toasted sandwiches to discover some sort of cheese with mushrooms and spinach, which was acceptable to both of them.

'Magnolia's going to make chocolates for our wedding,' Claire announced, squeezing Mark's thigh affectionately.

'Well, thank God for that. Maybe then she'll stop moaning about cowpat-cake-gate.'

'How dare you! I'd wallop you if you hadn't gone to the trouble of getting me a sandwich.'

Chapter Ten

As Magnolia's family and friends all went on their own version of a summer holiday depending on their preferences, returning with tans, tall tales and beatific looks on their faces, Magnolia switched up a gear in her efforts to get the shop ready for opening. Two weeks soon became three, and the shop moved closer towards resembling her dream.

As she was working in the shop front one day, Patricia close by, Magnolia's phoned buzzed on the hot chocolate counter. She picked it up, tapped a quick reply to the new message, and then looked up at Patricia, eyes shining. 'I have a surprise for you,' she announced.

Patricia's interest was immediately piqued. 'Is it something to do with your supermodel sister-in-law's car being illegally parked right outside the shop?'

'She's not a supermodel.' Magnolia rushed forwards. 'Meet us around the back,' she called over her shoulder to Patricia. 'On second thoughts... stay here and make sure no one wanders into the shop whilst the door is unlocked and we're unloading. I'll come and get you in a few minutes.'

Amazingly, Patricia did as she was asked and didn't even take a peek at what was going on outside. Little more than ten minutes later, Magnolia returned, secured the front door, and beckoned Patricia to the "garden that wasn't a garden", as they'd come to refer to it.

Though now it looked remarkably more like a garden. The square of grass had been edged on one side with six terracotta pots bursting with purple heather and lavender.

Patricia clapped her hands with excitement as her form rippled like a reflection in water, making Magnolia's eyes feel odd as she observed her reaction.

'The heather is for you, the lavender is for me,' Magnolia declared. 'Apparently, they get along well with each other.'

'You remembered, and you brought a slice of moorland to me!' Patricia skipped around like a sprite, 'Oh, you darling girl.' She stopped to gaze more closely at the colourful sprigs. Then she looked a little apologetic. 'You shouldn't make such grand gestures for me... I won't be here for much longer, and then it'll all seem like such a waste of your efforts.'

Magnolia gave an incredulous laugh. 'If it makes you happy whilst you are still here, however fleetingly that is, then it's totally worth it.'

Patricia beamed.

'Anyway, the heather is keeping the lavender company. I never even thought of growing my own lavender for making chocolate fillings with until now. So you've done me a favour by putting the idea into my head.'

Patricia fluttered right up close to the first terracotta pot. Then she promptly and neatly lay flat out on her back alongside it. Magnolia was mesmerised. It seemed so wholly unnatural that someone approaching their seventies could find this position with such ease; which it was, of course.

'Oh, come and join me?' Patricia implored. 'First, though… will you rearrange the pots? Just temporarily. If you put them in a tight semi-circle around my head, right in my line of sight, it'll really enhance the experience.'

Magnolia did so — both the pot re-arrangement, and the lying flat out on the floor.

They both lay in silence for a few heartbeats.

'It looks so majestic and all-encompassing from this perspective,' Patricia eventually said. 'I can pretend I'm actually on the moor. Imagine if a grouse came along and pecked my nose!' Her chortle was infectious. 'Or… imagine a charming little dry-stone wall meandering along to the left.'

'And if you were to raise your head, you'd see the undulating land falling away to the valley below like a giant's creased pillow after a long sleep,' Magnolia added — fully embracing Patricia's vision.

'Why would a giant have a purple pillow?' Patricia scoffed lightly.

'Why wouldn't he?'

A pair of rigger boots appeared. 'Am I disturbing something?' the male voice attached to them asked.

'Why do people ask that question, when it's obvious that they are?' Patricia grumbled.

It was the chandelier delivery guy. Even worse, he wasn't just delivering; he was also here to fit the damn thing.

'I'm just checking the height of the sprigs,' Magnolia said, forcing a casual tone. She sat up and then stood. *Christ, what an idiot I am. I really need to get better at switching from Patricia-world to the real world.*

'Wow, I didn't know gardening was so... intense.'

'Yes, it can be.' It was obvious that she had a lot of work to do if she was to dispel the weird atmosphere and reassure him that she wasn't a complete fruit-loop. It simply wouldn't do to have such a fiddly chandelier fitted by someone in a nervous frame of mind.

Better switch the fancy-pants drinks machine on, then.

'I'll stay here and monitor the height of the sprigs,' Patricia called gleefully after Magnolia, as she retreated into the shop with the chandelier guy in tow.

A couple of hours later, Raymond, the chandelier guy, had done his work to splendid effect and without any hiccups. As he'd now departed, to Magnolia's great relief, she decided a treat was appropriate and therefore wandered next door.

Her eyes scanned the counter appraisingly. 'Can't you start making *pain au chocolat*? I keep craving it, so it'd be very convenient if you did.'

'You know I don't do patisserie,' Jed said, with good-humoured, faux affront.

'*Pain* means bread, though.'

'Well, sweetbread has "bread" in its name too, and I don't do that, either. Do you know what it is? Offal. I don't think you'd want me to sell every product with "bread" in its title.'

'No, I suppose not.' Magnolia wrinkled her nose up in distaste.

'Why don't you try something from my veggie bread range? All the parents love me at the moment. I do a butternut squash and sage loaf that's really popular. And this beetroot and thyme *focaccia* is flying out the door!'

'Yep, go on, then,' Magnolia said, as Jed revealed the *focaccia* with a flourish. 'It does look amazingly tasty.'

Chapter Eleven

The late afternoon sun streamed through the shop windows, stretching across the wooden floor, just stopping short of where Magnolia sat at the hot chocolate counter. She'd obviously be getting blinds for the windows once she had her chocolates on display, to protect them from the changing temperatures, but for now, she could enjoy the luminescence.

She was boxing up whisky and vanilla truffles she'd made that morning for a posh corporate event — three of them per box, thirty boxes — when she sensed Patricia wandering over. She hadn't seen her today until now, which was unusual; being so busy earlier, she hadn't gone looking for her in the outbuilding.

'I notice your family and friends call you Nolly,' Patricia said. 'Which I think is ridiculous, by the way. Why would you want to shorten such a beautiful and sophisticated name to something so childish and bland? Just so you know, I'll only ever be calling you Magnolia. And heaven forbid… if you ever call me Pat, I'll curdle your truffles.'

Magnolia gave a short, surprised laugh. 'OK, good to know.'

Suddenly becoming subdued, Patricia floated onto the seat pad of one of the stools at the hot chocolate counter. Sensing she was about to say something significant, Magnolia stopped fussing with the ribbon she had been tying around a box of truffles and gave her full attention, trying not to appear overly intense.

'I know why I'm still here,' Patricia announced. 'I want to tell you about it; and also, the way that I died.'

Magnolia looked at her encouragingly and rested her elbows on the counter.

'My son, Nathan; he thinks he's responsible for my death.' Patricia paused, considering how best to compose her words. 'Before this place was your chocolate shop, before it was a pizza takeaway, or a shoe shop, it was an antiques shop. You know that already, but what you don't know is that it was *our* antiques shop — mother and son.

'I'm sorry to say that I wasn't entirely scrupulous in my antiques dealing. It was a constant cause of tension between us. Nathan has always been honest to a fault, and we'd have arguments time and time again about how much to charge for certain items; how best to describe them to potential customers. My only motivation was securing the maximum profit, even if that meant describing a piece as the genuine article when it was a poor copy. I never used to be like that… when and why did I become so horrid? Anyway, the business was really struggling, and whilst I had no compunction about charging a small fortune for a load of tat, Nathan became increasingly unhappy about it.

'One night, Nathan stayed late at the shop, doing the books. He ended up downing the best part of a bottle of whisky. I dropped into the shop to collect something and found him slumped over his desk, barely coherent. I took him home and ranted on at him for a good while before leaving him to his own devices.

'The next day he sent a text message saying he was sick and not coming to work — uncharacteristic, but hardly surprising given the circumstances the night before. Stewing in my own foul temper over the whole sorry situation we'd landed ourselves in, I trashed the place. No half measures, either — sixties-era sideboards and lamp-stands upended, vases and garden urns smashed. Then I just left it that way. It felt cathartic. I left the blinds down, left the *closed* sign flipped over. Sat down for a while to compose myself and half an hour or so later got up to make a cuppa.

'Next thing I know, I'm sprawled on the floor at an odd angle. Tripped over one of those damn ugly sideboards. Fractured hip, no less. Flashing lights, hospital… and here comes the terrible part. I blamed Nathan. My wonderful son, who found me and rescued me, who held my hand most of the way — that is, until I shook him off so harshly once I'd regained enough energy. I said that *he'd* trashed the place the night before — he just couldn't remember because of his drunken stupor. I said it was his fault that I'd tripped and fallen.

'Anyway, I went into the operating theatre with our relationship in a worse state than ever. They fixed my hip, but I caught an infection. A deadly infection, as it happens.'

Patricia sighed deeply, then stilled herself. She was so still that Magnolia wondered if she'd passed into some weird catatonic state particular to ghosts, if such a thing was possible. She'd been considering whether a hell of a lot of weird stuff was possible, lately.

She waited for her friend to continue. Patricia rubbed her eyes. This was the thing that really messed with Magnolia's head — the way she jumped between typical ghost behaviour and typical human behaviour — the manifestation of habits that she thought would have died along with her physical body.

Patricia continued.

'Then this is where things go totally bonkers. One moment I was leaving my body — floating upwards, as you'll have seen in the movies — and the next moment I opened my eyes, in so much as I thought I opened my eyes, to find myself here. In the shop.

'From that moment I knew I was dead. There was none of that slowly dawning realisation that you see in movies; I just knew it there and then. My body felt like smoke... how can I describe it... I was somehow everywhere and nowhere all at once. Well, not everywhere. Not like God. But somehow in the whole atmosphere of the shop. Every nook and cranny. But at the same time, I wasn't anywhere.

'Then, somehow, I pulled myself together. Strange phrase that, isn't it? I used to hate it when my mother used to say it to me as a young girl; somehow it didn't stop me using it myself when I had my own child, though. Never really used in a literal sense — I can finally use it that way, now.'

Magnolia smiled sympathetically, and quietly continued to listen.

'So, I pulled myself together and grounded in front of a hideous rococo-style full-length mirror. Of course, I was curious to see what I looked like. To see if I even had a reflection. And if I did, what sort of level of transparency had I been left with? I saw the same as what you can see of me, I guess. Semi-transparent, but enough to make out my features.'

There were a few moments of silence.

'So, what happened then? What happened to Nathan? How do you know that he blamed himself for you... dying?'

'Because I flat out told him it was his fault right before I died, didn't I? Can't get plainer than that. I told him it was his fault I fell, so it's not much of a leap for him to think it was his fault I got the infection that killed me. I wouldn't have been in hospital where I caught the infection if I hadn't fallen and needed surgery.

'Anyway, I don't know how much later it was — days, a week or so? — time's even more difficult for me to keep track of now. But he eventually came back to the shop; to clear it out and close the business. Game over in more ways than one. And of course, I was here when he came. Couldn't have been anywhere else, could I? He looked terrible, like he hadn't slept or eaten properly in days. No sparkle in him at all. And that's when my heart broke completely.'

'Have you seen him since?'

'No,' Patricia shook her head sorrowfully. 'He's never been back. When he was here that last time, I tried to catch his attention by moving a few things, but the best I could do in those days was make a few pages of a book flutter; nothing dramatic enough to stall him. And he obviously couldn't see me. I have no idea where he is now; he might have left the country, might have drunk himself to death like his feckless father did before him, for all I know.' This last bit ending on a sob, Patricia's form flickered a little at the edges; Magnolia noticed this happened whenever she was overcome by strong emotion.

'I could try to find him for you?' Magnolia suggested hopefully. 'We could try together to put it right?'

'Oh, that would be fantastic!'

'He must have social media accounts or some sort of online trail.'

Patricia's face fell. 'Actually, no. He's always been quite introvert. He always said he'd never succumb to all that malarkey.'

'OK. Well, he's probably still living wherever he was living when you were still alive. He'll probably have the same phone number, too.'

Patricia looked even more crestfallen. 'Damn, I can't remember his phone number.' She gazed into the distance as though trying to retrieve the magic digits. 'No, it's no good. Obviously, I do know where he lives, though. That's if he's still there.'

'Well, that's something.'

'Then what, though? If you do find him? What are you going to say to him? You can't just turn up at his house and tell him that his mother's ghost is haunting your shop, desperate to make amends.'

'Hmmm, that's true. We'll have to think of a plan to bring him here under false pretences. Then, once he's here, you can somehow announce yourself.'

'You can have a launch party! And invite him!'

'What, and then you're the *pièce de résistance* at the end? Right in front of a crowd of potential customers?'

'I suppose not. You could just *pretend* that you're having a launch party, though… and only invite him?'

'That's doable. So, we just need to think how to get to that stage.'

There was another moment of silence. A group of raucous teenagers walked past, and Magnolia caught the faint scent of fish and chips, vinegar and salt from the open window. It must be lunchtime.

'Did you have a website for your antiques business? Will it still be live?' Magnolia asked.

'We did, but even if it is still live, it won't make any difference. We didn't put our mobile phone numbers on there, only the shop landline.'

'Wow, that's a bit old-fashioned.'

'Well, it's quite fitting then, isn't it? For an antiques shop.'

'That's a ridiculous thing to say!' Magnolia laughed. 'It's like saying that because you had an antiques business, you did all your accounts with an abacus, parchment paper and a quill, instead of using a computer.'

Patricia bristled. 'I'm glad that you find my misfortune so entertaining.'

Magnolia became sombre again. 'I don't, really. I want to help you.'

Patricia suddenly perked up. 'There's a Louis XIV chair in the outbuilding!' she exclaimed, before doing a somersault in the air. The ribbons on the newly-wrapped gift boxes fluttered in the subsequent breeze.

'Huh?'

'Well... there's a *reproduction* Louis XIV chair in the outbuilding.'

'Please... can't you fast-forward a bit on this one? I don't know how it's relevant.'

'It's left over from when we had the antiques shop. Nathan must have forgotten to take it, but he'll want it for sure. We can use it as an excuse to reach out to him.'

'Oh, please don't tell me you want me to turn up at his house with it.'

Patricia beamed proudly.

'And what am I supposed to say? It's a bit of a weird thing to do. He'll wonder how I know his address, for a start. I can't tell him that the ghost of his mother told me where he lives. We need to save the freaky stuff for when we actually get him into the shop, remember.'

Patricia looked sad again, and Magnolia felt a pressing desire to do something meaningful in the interim, whilst they pondered a workable plan to entice her son to the shop. 'Does Nathan live locally?' she asked.

Patricia nodded. 'He lives just two miles away, before you come to Beraton village… just opposite that shop that sells flapjacks the size of a baby's head… if a baby's head was square, that is.'

'Without wanting to sound like a stalker… does he have any regular commitments or habits that result in him leaving the house at a specific time?'

'I wouldn't know, anymore. I wouldn't know what his habits are since he gave this place up.'

'Is he a sun lover, then? The weather's still hot at the moment. Is he likely to be sitting or working in his garden a lot? Can you see his garden easily from the street?'

'What are you getting at?' Patricia looked puzzled.

'I'm just thinking that I could check up on him for you. Until we think of a plan to bring him here, I could at least casually drive or walk past his house sometime when he's around the garden, cutting the grass or sunning himself... see if he looks healthy and happy? Would that make you feel better?'

'Yes!' Patricia rubbed her hands gleefully. 'A public footpath actually runs alongside his back garden. Y'know — one of those snickets. You could easily pretend you're going for a walk and have a little nose over the fence. I'd appreciate that so much, Magnolia!'

'No problem. What does he look like?' Magnolia was more than a little curious.

Patricia stretched out her arms, palms wide. 'I had plenty of photos of him, but they're all gone now, aren't they? And we didn't have photos of ourselves on the website, either.'

'You could describe him though,' Magnolia cajoled gently.

Patricia smiled deeply. 'He's an attractive man — but as his mother, I would say that, wouldn't I? And he's never spent time cultivating it or revelling in it, which is a bonus. I mean... he maintains all necessary hygiene standards, obviously. But other than that, he's wonderfully careless about his appearance.

'He has vivid, vibrant hazel eyes, which draw and then keep your attention, and a kind smile. He's tall, but not as tall as he seems — he just carries himself very well. His hair is atrocious — far too long and unruly, and defiantly dark streaked with silver, but I can let that go. He has an amazing bone structure — not sure where he got that from.'

'Does he — um — live alone, as far as you know? You didn't mention grandchildren or a daughter-in-law, but I just wanted to check. So I know what to look out for.'

Patricia looked surprised, and then resigned to the possibility. 'He was alone when I was alive. I guess he could be living with someone by now, but a wife and kids would be a fast-moving development. He's in his early forties now, but he's never settled down with someone longer than a couple of years. Eric and I probably didn't set a very good example of what a long-term relationship should be.' She sighed in contemplation.

'Well, I'll pass by his house when I leave here today — probably around four-thirty — to see what I can see,' Magnolia said encouragingly. 'Being a Saturday, he's probably more likely to be around.'

Arriving home a few hours later, only to promptly get into her car to drive to Nathan's street, Magnolia realised she hadn't done any driving in four weeks. Now that she worked little more than a kilometre from her home, it had become far less than a daily necessity. Could she remember how to actually drive?

It seemed so, thank goodness.

With due consideration for the locals, she parked innocuously on a grass verge, clear of driveways, just

111

before the street where Nathan lived, just to be extra cautious. She guessed she was about three-hundred metres away from his house, which seemed the perfect distance for a chance to cool down as she walked; the combination of hot weather and nervous anticipation had made her embarrassingly sweaty. Piling her hair on top of her head and securing it with a clip, before sweeping a tissue over the damp nape of her neck, she then swapped her ballet flats for trainers and set forth.

Contemplating the best way to conduct her surveillance without causing a stir, whilst also worrying whether she'd target the right house — to the *left* of the snicket, she reminded herself — meant she didn't realise there was a party going on until she was almost in the thick of it. Relaxed rather than raucous, it was a gathering of a dozen or so university-age youths — the main feature being an excessively smoking barbecue, and the purpose seemingly to soak up the sun, eat, drink and build an assault course from garden furniture for an eager spaniel.

Reminding herself not to become distracted and stick to the plan, loose as it was, Magnolia was about to hasten past, when she realised the party was actually happening at Nathan's house. Given the circumstances, Magnolia felt emboldened to directly enquire about the house owner. 'Is Nathan around?' she asked breezily. God knows what she'd say if he actually appeared.

A twenty-something returning to his sun-lounger from the barbecue screwed his face up in such exaggerated confusion that his sunglasses almost fell off. 'Who?'

Magnolia was temporarily mesmerised by his hair, which shot off in all directions. He looked as though he'd been caught in the force field of a landing helicopter. Was it intentional?

'The owner of the house,' the guy in charge of the barbecue clarified. He sauntered over, wiping his hands on a cloth. He was wearing a bright coloured, loose shirt with a bewildering print of tabby cats dressed in space suits. 'He's in Italy; has been for nearly a year. I think he's been renting this place out for nearly two years.'

'Oh, right.' Magnolia's face fell. 'Do you know if he's planning on coming back at some point?'

Weird-Shirt-Guy shrugged his shoulders. 'Dunno. We've been here for the last seven months, but we're just renting month-by-month. We're on a month's notice.'

'Hey, Max, we need more burgers!' someone shouted. There was a great clatter as a diminutive woman in a billowing red dress poured a sack-full of ice cubes into a plastic barrel full of beer bottles.

'Why don't you join us?' Weird-Shirt-Guy said, inclining his head towards the group. 'There's plenty of food and drink to go round.'

'No, thanks,' Magnolia smiled. 'There's stuff I need to do. Thanks anyway, though.'

At the end of the snicket, she glimpsed a charming little stile leading to a field of sheep, and beyond, a copse of fir trees on a hill. She decided to have a wander onwards; perhaps she'd be able to think of a gentle way of breaking the news to Patricia that her son had departed — his return any time soon uncertain.

Chapter Twelve

Patricia was inconsolable when Magnolia told her the next day what had transpired. Trying to put a positive spin on it, Magnolia suggested Nathan's retreat to Italy probably meant he was healing; at least he wasn't holed up in his house like a recluse. It didn't help, though. Wailing something about not even being able to cry properly because she didn't have tear ducts anymore, Patricia's image fuzzed around the edges repeatedly before she drifted off to the outbuilding.

Magnolia made a hot chocolate for Patricia to sniff and took it outside. There was no sign of her, until she peered through the outbuilding window and saw her sitting weirdly upright on the reproduction Louis XIV chair, in the centre of the gloomy interior, looking uncannily like a character in a Shakespeare play. Patricia had obviously thrown off the dust sheet shrouding the chair and dragged it into this more prominent position, because Magnolia definitely didn't recall it being visible when she'd had a quick nose around in there before — a piece of furniture as ornate and unusual as that wouldn't have gone unnoticed.

'I've brought you hot chocolate' she shouted, holding the mug up to the window.

'Go away! I don't want it!' Patricia replied petulantly.

'I'll leave it on the table in case you change your mind.' Magnolia duly placed the mug on the sun-bleached outdoor table and retreated to the shop.

At her laptop two hours later, she was just considering taking a break from working on her business plan, rolling her head back and forth to loosen the cricks in her neck, when she saw Mark approach the shop door. Patricia still hadn't ventured forth from the outbuilding, and this promise of some company was a welcome distraction from the intensity of her work. She gladly opened the door, and Mark barrelled in.

'I need chocolate,' he declared firmly.

Magnolia raised her eyebrows. 'Why?'

'Three cyclists have just turned up at the bike shop. They're in a bad way. They got a bit lost doing an epic ride, and ended up covering far too much distance on far too little food. One of them has hypoglycaemia. I said I'd bring him some chocolate to sort him out. The poor lad looks like he's going to pass out at any moment.'

'Oh, yeah?' Magnolia was instantly suspicious. 'So I guess you've completely sold out of your entire stock of fig and oat nutrition bars then? Plus, those special electrolyte thingies and special gels? That huge product range you have, dedicated to sustaining cyclists when they're on the move... you've completely sold out?'

Mark shrugged his shoulders sheepishly and looked everywhere except at Magnolia.

'Oh, for God's sake; just cut the bullshit and admit it's for you and your piggy mates and I'll get you something,' Magnolia said, a laugh softening her words. 'You do know that you're a terrible liar?'

'It's for me and my piggy mates,' Mark conceded, trailing her into the kitchen.

'Do you want white chocolate strawberry shortcake bites or dark chocolate maple pecan crisp?'

'Um... both,' he declared, grinning cheekily. She rolled her eyes and set about boxing up the treats.

'Wow, you're giving me two boxes full?'

'Yep. I want you to put one box on your sales counter for your customers to sample. Take some of my promotional flyers too. You only get chocolate for yourself if you promise you'll help promote my business.'

'OK, no problem!'

'I'll check with Rick whether you do it,' Magnolia warned, as they walked together back to the shop door, Mark evidently delighted with his stash. 'He wouldn't even dream of trying to lie to me.'

Much later, Patricia sidled up to the hot chocolate counter just as Magnolia was closing her laptop. 'I suppose you'll be off home in a bit,' she said forlornly.

Magnolia made a snap decision. 'How about I stay here and keep you company?'

A momentary spark lit Patricia's eyes, and then extinguished. 'Don't be daft. You can't stay here all

117

night. You need to recharge and refresh. And do all those things that humans do that are lost to me now.'

Magnolia shrugged. 'I could go home for a quick shower and change and be back here in an hour with some supplies to carry me through the night. How do you feel about a sleepover? You could tell me about all the great music from yesteryear that I've missed out on. It'll be fun.'

There was a beat as Patricia considered this, her head cocked to one side. 'It'll get cold as the night goes on. Do you have a sleeping bag?'

'Yep, it has extra insulation, to cope with the wintriest, wildest forests. It was quite expensive and I've hardly ever used it. You'd be doing me a favour. This way, I won't beat myself up about making a mistake in buying it and then not using it.'

'OK. That would be marvellous!' The edges of Patricia's form fluttered with excitement, like a flower in the breeze. She stilled and looked at Magnolia. 'Are you still here? Get going. The sooner you're gone, the sooner you'll be back.'

As promised, an hour later Magnolia returned to the shop with three bulging carrier bags and a rucksack. Patricia looked on in amazement as she revealed the treasures within: two lava lamps, one disco ball, two deflated space hoppers with a pump, a set of skittles and a light-weight bowling ball, two boxes of party poppers, a packed lunch box, a sleeping bag and a pillow.

'I thought we could put the music on and have a party,' Magnolia declared, eyes bright. 'I guess I'll be drinking that half empty bottle of tequila that's in the bottom kitchen cupboard without any assistance, but we can definitely create a fun ambiance with all this stuff. We can see if you have the dexterity to play skittles, and I know you won't be able to bounce on a space hopper yourself, but you could throw it at the walls a bit.'

It transpired that Patricia did indeed have the dexterity to play skittles; insofar as she couldn't actually wrap her fingers around the ball and throw it, but was instead able to will the ball towards the skittles with dramatic force through sheer concentration. The first time, the ball shot all the way across the shop floor, all the way across the kitchen floor beyond, and smacked into the back door with a great boom; six skittles capitulated — three each side. Magnolia thereafter made the wise decision to shut the adjoining door, pad the whole area with her sleeping bag and pillow, and place the skittles directly in front, to minimise potential damage.

They played two games comprised of ten frames, after which Patricia was declared the clear winner. High on her success, she then demanded that Magnolia let off five party poppers one after the other in celebration, before turning up the music.

After further consideration, throwing a space hopper at the walls was deemed too reckless and preposterous, but they pumped them up, and instead, raced each other from the shop front door to the kitchen back door; Magnolia bouncing on top of hers, Patricia shifting hers through force of will as with the skittles, although to make it fair, the rule was, she couldn't just slam it through the air, she had to make it bounce on the floor at least six times.

Magnolia won that competition, and took a celebratory swig of tequila. Then, as the tempo of the music became more energetic and the hands of the clock spun onwards, they danced joyously as though nothing else mattered.

At two o' clock in the morning, finally exhausted from dancing, bowling and bouncing, they sank to the shop floor, Magnolia snugly ensconcing herself in the sleeping bag, Patricia quite content on the bare floor. Actually, Magnolia considered, Patricia wouldn't even be depleted; she probably just appreciated the change in mood to something more sedate.

'Christ, Jed will be arriving next door soon. We'd better calm down and turn off the lights.'

'We've got a couple of hours yet.'

As Magnolia dragged the two lava lamps closer towards them — she found them extraordinarily relaxing, even just having them in the background — and began nibbling on her packed "beyond-midnight feast" of pita bread, hummus and olives, Patricia began to regale her with stories of her youth; in particular, her presence at Glastonbury in 1971.

As she talked, Patricia looked fondly at Magnolia, with her sleeping bag and Tupperware food box — reminders of the only two items she herself had taken to Glastonbury. She hadn't even taken a change of clothes. She'd been wearing an oversized caftan with a mind-bending concentric pattern, which had gradually and inexplicably deteriorated over the course of the festival, until it became a headscarf instead; thank goodness she was wearing shorts and a vest top underneath.

In that sparkling year of her twenty-first birthday, more by luck than great foresight and planning, she'd ended up at the Glastonbury Festival with Eric and three mutual friends. Except it wasn't the Glastonbury Festival. In those fledgling days — it was only its second year of being! — it was called the Glastonbury Fayre, and far from the behemoth it became, with less than twelve thousand attendees it was an altogether more surreal and inclusive experience.

The previous year, T Rex had replaced The Kinks at the last minute, and whilst they'd been a resounding success, there was nervous anticipation as to whether the same fate would befall this year's fayre, seeing as the plan was for David Bowie to perform. Well… maybe a markedly declining level of nervous anticipation, Patricia conceded, once the special "festival feeling" particular to those times had fully embraced everyone.

Her Tupperware box of sandwiches and fruit cake proved to be widely coveted, for there were no food

121

stalls at the festival back then. She'd kept the sandwiches for herself, but bartered the fruit cake for a selection of face and body paints.

She and her friends smeared every exposed inch of their skin in the vibrant coloured paint, thereafter resembling some breed of exotic mythical creature and challenging David Bowie — in his stage costume of sweeping magician's cape and weird floppy hat — for the accolade of most ethereal sight.

It may have been the result of poor planning, but for Patricia, Bowie's five o' clock in the morning slot was perfectly pitched. It was raw, intense and magical to experience his presence during that bewitching, just-around-dawn slice of time.

Many of the festival-goers were still sleeping when he began to perform, little pockets of them gradually emerging in dreamy wonder as the set unfurled. It was incredible in itself that Patricia was awake from the start; she couldn't even remember why she was, but it was by no means typical of her to rise so early.

And so it came to be, that on the marvellous morning of Midsummer's Day, Patricia was dancing in a dewy field as David Bowie sang *Changes* gloriously live, surrounded by sprite-like beings all emanating love and positive vibes.

'Wow, that sounds wonderfully otherworldly,' Magnolia declared, lolling her head dreamily. 'I love the way you tell your life stories. Your words take me right there. They really spark my senses.'

She leaned up on her elbow, and yet again, offered Patricia a plump, herb-infused olive. It was a sign of her increasing inebriation that she kept forgetting her friend was unable to eat; she'd also offered the tequila bottle several times. Or maybe it was more the case that their growing familiarity made it increasingly difficult for Magnolia to accept that Patricia was actually dead.

'Maybe it's because I'm obsessed with remembering sensory pleasure, now that I pretty much don't have any,' Patricia replied, looking pointedly from Magnolia to the olives and back again.

'Oops! Sorry, I keep forgetting,' Magnolia quickly and bashfully withdrew the olives. 'It's just that you seem so normal.'

'It's OK — don't worry,' Patricia smiled reassuringly. 'Now — I'm bored of talking about myself. Tell me, what's the weirdest commission you've ever taken on?'

'Oh, that's an easy one; chocolates for a historical battle re-enactment celebration banquet.'

Patricia raised an eyebrow. 'That sounds interesting. Tell me more.'

'Well, it was held deep in the forest, on Midsummer's Eve, funnily enough, this year. It was a crazy mash-up of medieval-meets-Arthurian-meets-Shakespearean-meets-Victorian times.'

'That's ridiculous! How did it work?'

'They just cherry-picked the best bits of each period to create an extraordinary party. First there was sword-fighting, then they had musicians playing lutes and bagpipes and drums and such-like as people danced along — all amongst the trees, of course. The costumes were mostly Arthurian; lots of sweeping, luxurious velvet and chainmail. There were blood-red candles dripping wax everywhere. I was so worried the trees would catch alight.

'There were five Guineveres and three King Arthurs. One of the Guineveres was with a jester, but one of the King Arthurs wanted to be with her instead. They were arguing, and it looked as though it was going to get violent, but then the King Arthur climbed a tree to avoid being punched by the jester, and didn't come back down until he was confident that the jester had drank enough mead and eaten enough pork and cranberry pie to have become disinterested.

'God knows what period the feast was from. They were drinking mead from wooden goblets, but also wine and beer from chunky faceted-glass goblets. There was a severed boar's head in the centre of the main table — which, as a pescetarian was really horrendous for me — as well as goose, pheasant, partridge… and venison. My contribution was three large fruit platters, which weren't really fruit platters.'

'What do you mean?'

'They were completely made from chocolate. Apples, grapes, pineapples, plums; the large "fruits" were just hollow chocolate shaped and coloured to mimic the fruit, but the grapes were truffles filled with a fruit-infused *ganache*.'

'That must have been disappointing, if someone just fancied a refreshing handful of proper grapes.'

'I know! Thankfully, though, the feedback I received was that everyone was pleasantly surprised. It's not as impressive as your Midsummer's Eve story, but there you have it.'

As Magnolia yawned and burrowed into her sleeping bag, pushing her snacks and bottle of tequila aside, Patricia returned to her reminiscences; privately, this time.

No wonder she missed the sensation of warm grass against her skin so much; it was all part of one of her fondest memories — kicking her sandals off to dance at Glastonbury. To say someone had "not a care in the world" was a cliché, but in retrospect, Patricia felt it was the one moment the phrase truly described her emotional state.

Since 1971 she'd returned to Glastonbury a further three times, and although none of those experiences reached the heady heights of her first festival, they were still memorable for all the right reasons.

Why had she stopped going? She could fool herself into believing it was the birth of Nathan that had instigated her metamorphosis into sensible, twinset-and-pearls-wearing Patricia — who shuddered at the thought of sleeping on bare ground beneath the stars, spontaneously going where her mood took her or

kicking her shoes off to dance at every opportunity —
but she knew in her heart that wasn't true.

The change began two years earlier, when Eric
started channelling all his time and energy into making
as much money and drinking as much alcohol as
possible. The subsequent decades-long disenchantment
that overcame Patricia meant she didn't even want to try
to convince Eric to return to Glastonbury — they'd both
evolved too far from who they were then, and going
back to the festival would taint her precious memories
and only serve to accentuate what she'd lost.

Whilst she regretted not celebrating her youth
more, what would she actually do if she had her life
back at her current age? Could she honestly say she
would do all the fantastical things that she was yearning
for now as a ghost? Free from aches and pains, coughs
and sniffles, fatigue and temperature discomfort,
physical hunger and thirst, as she now was, it was easy
for her to see herself taking on all manner of adventures.

But what she felt she was missing out on was a
skewed version of reality.

Take camping beneath the stars, for example. It
wouldn't all be hot, fragrant soup and toasted
marshmallows around a cosy, crackling open fire; the
gambolling flames competing with the splendid sky for
the best of her attention. Lying back on the forest floor
to watch the stars wouldn't feel like being caressed by
foliage with feathers-and-fur softness.

It would be cold, the ground would be hard and probably damp, and she'd likely still be hungry if she'd eaten only soup and marshmallows. And just as she settled into a comfortable position, she'd need to get up to urinate. Oh, and the insect bites! She'd probably be horrendously itchy as a result of those.

In short, she was remembering all the sensory joys of being human and forgetting the discomforts and hardships. And those discomforts and hardships heightened and multiplied with old age.

So... the question was: having left her life at the age of almost seventy, did she really want to return to her body if she could only return where she left off, at that age?

Damn right she would. Well, tough luck. Things could be a lot worse; and had been, until Magnolia arrived.

'Oh, I wish we were under a starry night's sky,' she said aloud, tilting her head back.

As it had been a while since either of them had spoken, lost as Patricia had been in her reverie, when Magnolia jolted to attention and stared at her —quite a funny effect, seeing as she was swaddled so snugly in her sleeping bag, looking rather like a caffeine-crazed giant caterpillar — Patricia thought it was because she'd woken her.

'Patricia, you're a genius!'

'Of course I am.'

'No, I mean — that's what I'm going to do! I'm going to paint a starry night's sky on the ceiling!' Magnolia looked up at the pleasingly pristine yet undeniably plain shop ceiling. 'It'll set everything off perfectly.'

'You'll have to do it properly. A slapdash effort will just look ridiculous.'

Magnolia spluttered on a swig of tequila. 'Oh, don't hold back, will you? Don't you have faith that I'll do a proper job?'

Patricia softened. 'Yes, of course. Looking at your track record, I have to say, I'm impressed. It's extraordinary what you've achieved so far, just with the look of this place. And that's even before you've filled it with chocolate.'

'I won't do it by myself. I'm not delusional. There was a guy helping us to paint the old water tower who's a talented artist. I'll ask him to do it.'

And with that, Magnolia promptly settled back down.

'Thank you, my dear,' Patricia whispered, noticing Magnolia finally drifting into sleep. 'Who knew there could be life after death? You've brought me unexpected joy and friendship during these in between months.'

Chapter Thirteen

When Magnolia woke a few hours later, Patricia had vanished.

But Jed had appeared.

Loud as it was, the knocking on the shop door was muffled somewhat by the steady, tequila-induced thumping in her head. Seeing it was Jed from her position on the floor, she hoped he couldn't likewise see her. She struggled to disentangle herself from her sleeping bag, but eventually, her legs carried her to the door, and she answered.

He looked bemused, but also relieved.

'I thought you were being burgled!' he exclaimed. He noticed the lava lamp on the floor by Magnolia's sleeping bag, and pointed at it. 'That glow was reflecting off your counter and I thought it was a burglar's torch; especially because it keeps bobbing up and down.'

She took a step backwards and tried not to breathe too heavily, remembering that she hadn't brushed her teeth after her night-time picnic and booze fest. 'Thanks for checking,' she said, forcing a brightness she definitely didn't feel. 'As you can see, though, I was just making my overnight stay in the shop more interesting, and… seventies themed.'

Clearly, he wasn't sure what to say to this. 'Erm… why?' He looked around, taking in the evidence of the previous night's party. 'Skittles aren't seventies,' he added.

'Yeah, I got that bit wrong, I suppose.' She looked down at her mint green pyjamas, and decided they were just about respectable. 'It's a new creative development technique I read about somewhere; immersing yourself completely, over the course of several hours, in the specific theme that you want to channel into your product.'

'And you want to channel the seventies era into your chocolates?'

Christ, the things I say and do to avoid mentioning your existence, Patricia.

'There's a specific off-shoot range I'm considering, which would be loosely inspired by the seventies, yes.'

'Wow. Maybe I should try that creative development technique for new bread ranges. I'm looking for a bit more oomph.'

He stepped back from the doorway. 'Anyway, you're obviously not in danger, or being burgled, so I'll leave you to it. Next time, try drinking a snowball, though.'

He walked away before Magnolia had the chance to respond. She stood there for a couple of minutes afterwards, wondering how and why anyone would want to drink a snowball, and whether it was in some way related to behaviour in the seventies.

Finding Patricia in the outbuilding (in much better spirits — it seemed the impromptu sleepover party had worked) she informed her that she needed a few hours recuperation and that she'd be back later in the afternoon.

After a couple of hours' much-needed extra sleep, she went for a run to cleanse herself further of the night's excesses.

Deciding that she could only manage a gentle pace and telling herself that this was fine, it was good enough just to be getting some fresh air, she was pleased to discover that once she started moving and the endorphins started flowing, she was in the mood to push it a little further than intended.

Leaping over a ford, running past the delightful old vicarage with the steeply pitched roof that she often fantasised fairy tales about, she endured the subsequent hill, before being rewarded for her efforts at the top with a view of the town below and a pleasing sense of wellbeing.

As she ran on, her legs and cardiovascular system more able to maintain a steady rhythm with the now flat terrain, the niggling puzzle of how to drink a snowball unravelled. She realised it must be a cocktail. Of course, she should have just asked Patricia. She felt the kiss of light rain on her face, but it was OK; she was nearly home now, and at its current tempo it was rather refreshing.

That afternoon, back at the shop, Patricia was back to her inquisitive self.

'What are you nosing out the window at?'

'A double-decker bus has just stopped at the traffic lights. It looks quite fancy, though. It's painted *eau de nil* and the windows seem to have damask silk curtains.'

Magnolia came over to look, whistled through her teeth at the stylishness of the bus, and then noticed the name painted extravagantly on the side. 'It's The Whirly Wanderer!' She clapped her hands three times in rapid succession and danced a little jig on the spot.

'Well... I thought it was interesting, but I wouldn't have thought it was *that* exciting.'

'It's one of those pop-up restaurants,' Magnolia enthused. 'Well, not exactly. It travels around the UK, only stopping in one place for around four nights per year. I'm eating there tomorrow evening with Beth and Dan. It's stopping at the centre of Serrel Wood, in that glade that always seems to have a gorgeous, gold-emerald light all around.

'Obviously, space on board is limited, so they can't offer an extensive menu. We had to order in advance from just two choices of starter, main course and dessert. I'm having scallop *cerviche* with pomegranate, then *miso*-marinated salmon with ginger and rhubarb salad and glass noodles, then orange blossom honey and *yuzu* chocolate mousse cake.'

'Whoop-di-doo. Meanwhile, I'll be sat in the outbuilding, eating dust and seeing how many birds I can scare off the windowsill over the course of the evening.'

'Oh, don't be like that! I'd invite you along, if I could. Shall I take some photos? Would you like that, or would it just make it worse?'

'Photos would be nice,' Patricia said, softening her attitude somewhat. 'Take at least a couple of each course, please. And I'd like to see some photos of the bus interior, as well as its position in the glade. I don't want any photos of your friends in full gurning mode, though.'

''They don't gurn! No problem, though.'

At that moment, Mark burst into the shop, his eyes alight. 'The Whirly Wanderer was just at the traffic lights! Did you see it?'

'Yes! I'm so excited!'

'I'm so jealous that you're eating there.'

'Oh, Christ Almighty, you're like a couple of kids.' Patricia shook her head and sloped away.

Chapter Fourteen

'Oh, let's give up the farm and follow this magic bus all around the country,' Beth declared dreamily, swallowing a marvellous morsel of sesame seared tuna and leaning back in her seat rapturously.

'What about Dominic?'

'He can come with us. We just have to leave the cows behind.'

'I meant what about his schooling?'

'Oh, Dan! It's just a fantasy. You don't have to ruin it with practicalities.' She shared a look of solidarity with Magnolia and took a sip of wine. Magnolia took a flurry of photos as unobtrusively as possible, before focusing her attention on her starter.

The smooth, milky and salty flavour of the scallops blended perfectly with the sweet, crisp burst of the pomegranate seeds. It looked so beautiful on the plate, too, like something created by a garden fairy; thinly sliced bright white scallop discs arranged like flower petals, the scattering of pomegranate seeds like precious rubies, with a pop of green from a flourish of micro cress. Magnolia would have felt compelled to take photos anyway, regardless of Patricia's request.

She looked around contentedly as she ate. The tables were dressed with snappy linen cloths with a tiny vase of fresh wildflowers at the centre of each one, and the crockery and glassware were fine and elegantly shaped. The pattern on the plates and the stems of the wineglasses was *art nouveau* in style, which was in keeping with the woodland surroundings. And no one here could forget those woodland surroundings. At every window, the trees seemed to tap at the glass, imploring to be granted entry. It was sublime. There was just the right amount of happy background buzz from fellow diners, and the owners were attentive yet breezily so; they were certainly not overwhelming.

Their empty starter plates were whisked away, and all three of them rested their elbows informally on the table. Magnolia was wearing a three-quarter sleeve blouse in a romantic tea rose shade, cut through with threads of bronze, and the sleeves shimmered pleasingly as the glow from hundreds of tiny, well-placed lights that flickered around the bus interior bounced off them.

Magnolia's salmon main course arrived. It was sensational, and in taking her time to savour it fully, she found she had to fiercely protect half of it from being stolen by Dan.

'Do you think they'll let us in the kitchen?' Dan suddenly mused, eyes bright.

'No. Why would they?'

'It's a thing they do now, isn't it? Encouraging customers to see what goes on behind the scenes; a chance to show off a bit. Lots of restaurants have open kitchens now… or a "chef's table" for a party of lucky diners.'

'Dan, they're not going to let you in the kitchen here. They're far too busy right now, and more pertinently, there'll barely be enough room to swing a cat in a kitchen built into a double-decker bus just when the two owners are in it, without you blundering about in there as well.'

'Oh, now who's killing off fantasies?' They all laughed companionably.

Their desserts arrived. Beth had chosen the orange blossom and *yuzu* chocolate mousse cake along with Magnolia. 'Wow, you really should come up with a chocolate that incorporates these flavours,' she said, curling her spoon over her bowl to reach the last slither.

A self-possessed woman in a well-cut, grey brocade trouser suit at the next table inclined towards them with interest. 'Are you a *chocolatier*?' She addressed Magnolia, rather directly. Her eyes were unflinching and inquisitive as she swirled her cognac, which was in a wonky — by design — glass tumbler; the effect was dizzying.

Magnolia told her about her current situation and status, and with Beth interjecting at every opportunity she could find to sing the praises of her friend, plus the sharing of her website, which already had a varied and impressive gallery of photos showcasing her chocolates, Magnolia soon found herself accepting a commission to provide six-hundred chocolates for the mayor's prestigious upcoming annual garden party.

'I knew it would come down to chocolate in the end,' Dan said, playing at being long-suffering, as they moved outside The Whirly Wanderer to wait for their taxi.

'You should be happy that Magnolia got some good business out of the evening,' Beth admonished him. 'And it's not as though she actually sought it out. The mayor approached her.'

'I know, I'm just using it as a prelude... to suggesting we climb one of those trees over there whilst we wait for the taxi.'

'What are you on about? We're not climbing any trees,' Magnolia declared primly.

'It'll be fun! And there'll be a cracking good view from the top,' Dan cajoled.

'No. What will the mayor think if she sees us? And we'd have to tuck our skirts into our knickers.'

'And you shouldn't climb trees after drinking alcohol,' Beth added — clearly on Magnolia's side. 'Or, if you're over the age of thirty.'

'You should only climb trees if an angry jester is chasing you.'

'What?' Beth and Dan said in unison — both bewildered by Magnolia's bizarre scenario.

'It's a long story. And it's also chocolate-related; a theme which Dan has already voiced his displeasure about as taking up too much of his time.'

'And the taxi is here now, anyway.' Beth dipped her head towards the approaching vehicle.

Chapter Fifteen

The several hours' drive from Bruges had done little to diminish Mathias' rage; if anything, it had made him even more incandescent. An astonishingly bad full English breakfast at a service station was repeating on him, and he could still taste the bitter, too-hot coffee that had accompanied it on his tongue. The two fleeting, inadequate rest stops had left his eyes gritty, and his head felt full of treacle whenever he moved it too quickly.

He hadn't intended to face-off with Magnolia immediately upon returning to the UK from Bruges — he'd made Newcastle his home several years ago — but the events of the last few days now compelled him to do so, and Magnolia's town was en route anyway.

Switching his car engine off, he checked his phone, where he'd stored Magnolia's current address details, as copied from his mother's address book, to make sure he was in the correct street.

Walking up the path to Magnolia's front door, he noticed the garden was rather tiny yet tidy, though the stepping stones were rather wobbly. Not good if she still favoured stiletto heels. The green front door looked recently painted, and had a brass door knocker in the shape of a pineapple. How ridiculous.

'Hello, dear,' an age-cracked voice said from behind him, just as he was about to knock. He turned to see an old woman with a Bichon Frise gambolling around her ankles, the contrast serving to accentuate her frailty. 'Are you looking for Magnolia?'

He nodded. 'Yeah. Do you think she'll be in?'

'I doubt it, dear. She'll probably be at her chocolate shop.'

'Ah, of course; on the High Street, right?' he bluffed, hoping he'd guessed correctly and that the woman wouldn't become suspicious of his lack of familiarity with Magnolia's whereabouts these days.

'That's right,' the woman confirmed, swaying unsteadily on her feet as her dog tugged on his leash. 'She has the shop sign up now. It looks very elegant, I must say.'

'Great. Thanks for your help,' Mathias said quickly, before she could launch into full conversation mode. As he returned to his car, he tried to appear relaxed rather than aggressive. He didn't yet know how he was going to deal with his issue, but something would come to him.

Magnolia adored the oak floorboards in her shop; after some deliberation, though, she decided they were too pale, and that she was going to varnish them to a richer, dark honey colour.

Seeing her arrive in jeans and plaid shirt that morning, armed with tins and various sized brushes, Patricia had gawped at her appearance — jeans were an unusual choice for Magnolia — and looked momentarily excited, before deeming the primary task of the day far too boring for her attentions and floating outside for some fresh air. Relishing the rare peace, Magnolia flipped open the blinds to let in the sunlight, made herself a cappuccino, and set forth.

She soon found that brushing the varnish on was an unexpectedly enjoyable task. It was almost like working with melted chocolate, but without the stress of having to strictly control the temperature and work within a specific time period. She was in a wonderful zen-like state, the sun from the window warming her face, when the vibe of the morning thus far suddenly took a nasty turn.

The masculine shadow at the door alerted her first, before the aggressive thump of him knocking for entry reverberated through the shop. Hurriedly placing the varnish brush on the upturned tin lid, she stood from her kneeling position, wiped her hands on a rag, and opened the door.

It was Mathias. And he looked furious.

Taken aback — she hadn't seen him for four years and only then because his father had died and she wanted to pay her respects at the funeral — she allowed him into the shop.

This was a big mistake.

'So, butter-wouldn't-melt Magnolia manages to screw me out of my inheritance,' he sneered, grabbing her elbow roughly with one hand and slamming the door with the other.

'What? I don't know what you're talking about,' she stammered, trying to break free. He let her go, but remained far too close, looming over her. His face looked unpleasantly greasy and doughy, as though he'd been eating all the wrong things and not been taking care of himself properly.

'I'm talking about my mother leaving all the money from the sale of my parents' business to you.' Seeing the astonishment on her face, he backtracked a little. 'Did you know that she left it all to you in her will?'

'Her will? Has Agnes died?' Magnolia responded in dismay.

'She died of bowel cancer two weeks ago,' he responded harshly.

There was a pause.

'I'm sorry, I didn't know,' Magnolia finally uttered, slumping against the wall. 'I knew she'd had breast cancer… I didn't know it had spread… I thought they'd caught it in time. She never said anything in her letters.'

Magnolia and Agnes had maintained their friendship in the years since she'd first visited Bruges as Mathias' girlfriend, exchanging letters the old-fashioned way on a regular basis. Largely revolving around their shared passion for chocolate, their missives

142

had always conveyed the mutual admiration and affection they held for each other; Magnolia was forever appreciative of Agnes and Frederick's patient tutelage and the opportunities they'd given her, enabling her to set out on the path to a sparkling future as a *chocolatier*; Agnes, and Frederick, were enchanted by Magnolia's enthusiasm, and always remembered her dedication and generosity in helping them through that long-ago busy summer.

Shocked and upset, Magnolia struggled back to an upright position and laid a consoling hand on Mathias' arm. 'I'm really sorry for your loss, Mathias,' she said gently.

He shook her hand away angrily. 'Sorry for my loss, but happy for your gain, eh?'

Magnolia was confused — the revelation of Agnes' death had momentarily made her forget Mathias' original words — then she remembered what he'd said about her "screwing him out of his inheritance".

'Mathias, I…'

He didn't wait to hear what she had to say on the matter. Storming through to the kitchen, Magnolia hot on his heels, he surveyed the bounty laid out on the worktops with a manic gleam in his eye. 'I see it's all going pretty damn fantastic for you now that the money's pouring in,' he spat out.

Magnolia had spent the best part of three days making chocolates, with a liquid caramel and Cornish sea salt centre, for the mayoral event. The most demanding part of the project had been shaping the chocolates like maple tree leaves, as requested by the mayor; it was a painstaking process that had left her with a crick in her neck and numb fingers, yet also a marvellous sense of achievement.

The chocolates were now laid out on five gleaming trays, ready to be boxed up, intricate, leaf-like shells glossy and tempting.

Mathias picked one up and stuffed it into his mouth. Magnolia looked on nervously. 'Delicious,' he declared, his voice thick with caramel. The he reached out, grabbed five of them in his fist, and threw them to the floor.

'Mathias, please don't!' Magnolia cried, planting herself between her ex-boyfriend and the fruits of her labour. Pushing her roughly aside, in one triumphant stroke, he swept all five trays onto the floor. 'Oh, my God! Why did you do that?' Magnolia looked in horror at the broken tumble of chocolates oozing their centres, back up at Mathias' grinning face, and back down at the increasingly sticky mess on the floor.

He shrugged nonchalantly. 'I'm sure you can afford to make more.'

As a spike of angry tears welled, Magnolia saw him survey the rest of the kitchen, looking for further opportunity to wreck maximum destruction. His eyes alighted on a nearly full bottle of Jamaican rum that she used in truffles, and he grabbed it victoriously, holding it aloft as though it was the Olympic torch, before loosening his grip to send it smashing to smithereens.

'*How dare you*!' Patricia's voice suddenly boomed forth. Magnolia jumped, but Mathias' reaction was even more pronounced. He instantly stopped his rampage and swivelled full circle on the spot, his eyes darting all over the place.

'Where the hell did that come from?' he exclaimed. He looked at Magnolia for enlightenment. She shrugged, watching Patricia's approach from the corner of her eye without turning her head. In a quick jerk, Patricia elevated an aluminium mixing bowl and sent it slamming into Mathias' face.

The force sent him stumbling backwards, mercifully away from the shards of broken glass, before he crashed to the floor. The mixing bowl bounced merrily out of the kitchen and into the shop. Magnolia brought her hand to her mouth in fright as she observed a trickle of blood dripping from his forehead onto the crushed chocolate mess around him.

'He'll be fine,' Patricia reassured her, swooping over to take a closer look. 'It was only aluminium. I'd have used the granite mortar if I'd intended to kill him.'

Sure enough, he soon stirred. As his eyes focused and his limbs twitched, Patricia sent a two-litre jug of water cascading over his prone body, quashing any misconception he might have that Magnolia was responsible for the attack and instilling a profound fear instead, as he realised some other mysterious force was at play.

He scuttled to his feet surprisingly quickly given his trauma, almost slipping back down again as a result of the small puddles of water encircling him. 'Some fucking crazy shit going on here,' he declared, terror and incomprehension sending his voice an octave higher, as he backed cautiously out of the kitchen. Having made it into the shop without suffering a further blow, he ran to the door — straight through the still-wet varnish — and ejected himself into the street with impressive speed.

Taking in the footprints defacing her newly varnished shop floor, and the chocolate and rum gloop spiked with shards of glass in the kitchen, Magnolia stood on the threshold between the two and began to sob wretchedly.

Patricia tried to touch her shoulder consolingly, remembered she couldn't, and subsequently buzzed around indecisively like a bumble bee, trying to find a way to provide physical comfort. She finally settled beside Magnolia in an odd crouching position, her head cocked at an unnatural upward angle, so that she could make eye contact whilst accommodating Magnolia's downward gaze. 'Please don't cry, dear. It'll all be OK.'

'How will it be OK?' Magnolia cried beseechingly. 'He's ruined everything. I was on a knife edge, anyway. Those chocolates he smashed up were for a very important client with massive influence. There's no way

I can avoid letting her down now... my reputation is going to be ruined.

I'm just so tired of it all. I can't do this anymore. I shouldn't have got carried away with all these fantastical ideas that are beyond my ability to execute. I should just go home and start looking for another office job, something safe and steady.'

'You can't let that nasty bully win!' Patricia declared firmly. 'It's not always going to be rosy and cosy with this new venture of yours. But you've got to find the strength to push through the difficult times, and have belief that you'll come through it, back to the rosy, cosy times; because you will. I know you will. I can see the potential in you.'

Unfortunately, Patricia's words fell on deaf ears.

Chapter Sixteen

Magnolia stayed at the shop just long enough to clean up the mess Mathias had created — whilst Patricia hovered in the background, powerless to help, yet trying to offer words of encouragement — before heading home in defeat.

She couldn't summon the strength or imagination required to come up with an alternative product for the mayor's party so, instead, simply phoned her to say that she regretfully couldn't honour the order. She couldn't even remember the excuse she'd concocted; it was all a bit of a blur. Then she switched off her phone, changed into pyjamas, and crawled into bed, blocking out the world with her duvet.

The following three days were largely spent shuffling around the house in an over-sized dressing-gown, eating tomato soup and leftover roast potatoes, and watching old Audrey Hepburn movies, all in a fuzz of lethargy brought about by a combined lack of fresh air, exercise and hope.

When she ran out of Audrey Hepburn movies to watch, she stumbled upon a documentary about a billionaire who'd made his fortune through unrevealed means, and had subsequently built ten luxury tree houses in ten different countries. It was such a bizarre story, that having watched it and promptly fallen asleep on the sofa afterwards to be assailed by weird dreams, she wondered when she woke up whether it had been a real documentary at all or just a construct of her fevered imagination.

She discovered that her next-door neighbour's cat paid far too much attention to her garden, that the postman delivered the post between ten-thirty and ten-thirty-five every day and, most surprisingly, that she missed Patricia's casual commentary — whether it be charming or cutting — much more than she thought she would.

Some hours later, having just consumed a whole bottle of *Chablis*, she had a vague memory of answering the phone to Claire and then Mark, both concerned about her whereabouts. She told them that she was sick of trying to live up to other people's expectations. They both told her that the expectations were all in her own head, and generally seemed quite bewildered by her behaviour. She couldn't seem to reach through the dense syrup of her own thoughts to extract and articulate an explanation for how she felt, so she muttered something wholly inadequate instead and put the phone down.

Mathias' destructive outburst in her shop brought the memory of a similar experience from childhood to the forefront of her mind; its visual vibrancy faded with age, yet its emotional impact still resonant. When she'd spoken to Mark, she could sense that he was remembering the same incident.

Magnolia had been seven years old, which would have meant Mark was nine years old. In a fit of exuberant indulgence born from a romantic anniversary weekend away, their mother had bought them each an extraordinarily elaborate Belgian chocolate Easter egg. As well as the superior quality chocolate shell, Magnolia's egg was decorated with a cascading pattern of around forty individual, intricate flowers in pink, white and yellow. She adored it.

For almost two weeks she had it displayed on top of the cabinet in the family dining room; it gradually acquired a cluster of companions as aunties, uncles and grandparents also gifted her and her brother with eggs. She could often be found gazing at it, mesmerised, having been on her way to the kitchen or her bedroom, her purpose in going to that room now forgotten.

Then one day, a friend of Mark's, Gareth Edgar, called round for tea after school. A bully of a boy, prickling with barely contained spite and restless energy, he immediately honed in on the Easter eggs — in particular, Magnolia's floral, Belgian wonder and Mark's equally impressive version decorated with stars.

'Giz a closer look at that,' he demanded, pointing at Magnolia's egg, his eyes glinting with wicked intent. Magnolia and Mark looked at one another with nervous foreboding.

'We're not allowed to touch them at all until Easter weekend,' Mark told him.

This only served to add fuel to the fire; for Gareth promptly helped himself, plucking the egg from its position and tossing it carelessly from one hand to the other. 'I wonder if it would bounce if I dropped it,' he said, grinning hatefully.

He threw it back and forth with increasing mania, its airborne arc higher each time, taunting them, until it finally smashed against the wall, falling to the floor as a cardboard-cellophane-chocolate mess.

After the initial shock, Magnolia felt a flutter of hope in her chest — it was still salvageable. He'd ruined its beauty and stolen the sense of anticipation and subsequent pleasure she'd have had cracking open the shell, but it was still edible. It had broken into only a few shards, and it was still in its box.

Until he raised his foot and brought it mercilessly down on his target.

The cellophane window popped open, and some of the now smaller pieces flew out.

Magnolia truly believed he would have actually ground the chocolate into the carpet, but that would have revealed his true nature to their parents, so he didn't. Instead, he grabbed the vase of drooping daffodils that was arm's length away on the table, and up-ended it onto the chocolate remains. The water from the vase had a brown tinge and smelt of decay, for the daffodils were well on their way out.

When their mum asked what had happened, he pretended that he'd accidentally fallen forwards, hitting the table, whilst Magnolia had been offering the egg to him for a closer look, both egg and vase becoming victims of his clumsiness.

As neither Magnolia nor Mark made a big fuss, Gareth ended up staying for tea as planned. They had fish tacos served help-yourself style, complete with their mum's homemade spice-rub and salsa, of which Gareth snatched far more than his fair share. Magnolia could still recall how his greedy fingers grabbed at the food like convulsing starfish.

Afterwards, just before his mum arrived to collect him, Gareth was struck on the forehead by an airborne pencil tin whilst in Mark's room.

He never returned.

Mark had shared his star-strewn Belgian chocolate egg with her — he'd keenly suggested it himself, without any cajoling from their mum — and being Magnolia's first taste of Belgian chocolate, it had been a revelation. It was the taste equivalent of playing ten rippling notes on her dad's piano, having repeatedly struck just one note for far too long. She still smarted at Gareth's wanton will to deprive her of her own egg, though.

A couple of weeks later, Magnolia and Mark had been tasked with setting the table for a family roast dinner, when Mark discovered a tiny white sugar flower, still intact, on the seat cushion of one of the dining room chairs. Magnolia saw him pause, his head dipped, a fork brandished in mid-air, before he retrieved the sugar flower between thumb and forefinger and dropped it gently into his sister's palm.

She kept it on her dressing table, nestled between her collection of fruit-shaped-and-scented soaps and cold-cast bronze dolphin ornament, only throwing it away weeks later when her mum warned her that it would attract mice.

Not yet ready to pull away from self-pity, Magnolia poured another glass of wine.

Rather inconveniently, somewhere along the way, everyone seemed to have abandoned the notion of the shop being haunted, except the newly terrorised Mathias, of course. Mark told her, during yet another phone call, that he'd actually seen Mathias approaching the chocolate shop; not noticing anything odd about his demeanour, and being otherwise engaged advising a potential customer on the benefits of chamois cream, he'd merely made a mental note to ask her about it later, rather than nosily coming over, as his character would usually dictate.

He'd accepted his sister's re-telling of events — that Mathias had trashed the place in a fury over his mother's will — which was true, of course, save for Patricia's contribution to ousting the bully. Afterwards, though, Magnolia considered it would have been better to lead her brother to believe the whole incident had been the work of a poltergeist. At least then no one would be haranguing her to return, as they now were.

She decided she should cut her losses and get out now, whilst the money, time and energy she'd invested was minimal. But what about the heart she'd invested? Better not to think about that. She felt sure she could convince Mark to take the hot chocolate bar, complete with drinks machine. He had the space in the bike shop, and he'd frequently talked of installing a refreshments station before she'd taken on her shop. He'd only pulled away from the idea once Magnolia was doing it. Plus, she could still take on special requests for family and friends, and use up her current stock on these.

What about her magnificent steampunk-inspired shelving? There was no reason why she couldn't bring it home and use it in her kitchen or living room instead — for crockery or books, she considered.

With no one around to temper her skewed judgement, she then became rather maudlin about the "fact" that no one wanted her. She started thinking of the redundancy from her office job as a personal rejection, and her few failed romantic relationships suddenly took on a new slant, whereby she completely forgot that she hadn't wanted to stay in each relationship, anyway.

On the fourth day, she washed her hair, dabbed on a smattering of make-up and changed into a smart black pencil dress with matching patent leather ballet flats. The brilliant sun, which had been striking the windows beseechingly, was finally granted entry; and the letter from the executor of Agnes' will lay opened, read, and ultimately discarded on the console table by the front door; it had been waiting for her when she returned from the shop on the day of Mathias' rampage.

Pausing for a moment on the doorstep to take a cleansing breath of jasmine-scented air, her eyes and brain re-configuring as they dealt with the stimulus of the real world again, Magnolia then walked purposefully towards the High Street and an advert she recalled seeing in a restaurant window for a waitressing vacancy.

She was given a trial shift that very evening, and before she knew it, had worked four evenings in a row. On the fifth morning, still in bed at ten o' clock — having endured a hen party the night before that lingered far too long and expelled gold glitter all over the table and floor — she was harshly woken by someone hammering at the door. Hurriedly yanking her dressing gown on, she stumbled to answer it.

It was her mother. And she didn't look happy.

'What the hell are you doing here?' Magnolia asked.

'Well, that's just charming! What the hell are *you* doing here?'

'I live here.'

'Yes, but why aren't you at the shop?'

'It didn't work out. I've got a waitressing job now, whilst I figure out what to do next. You've just woke me up — last night was crazy. I was pouring *prosecco* and battling rogue glitter until gone midnight.'

'Are you *serious?*'

'Yep. It was a hen party.'

The vein at Lauren's temple throbbed. 'You know exactly what I mean, Magnolia Aitken,' she enunciated in angry staccato. 'Now let me in.' Magnolia sighed, and gestured for Lauren to enter. She felt sure her parents had only given her an excessively long name so that they could shorten it, but then use the full-on version to full effect when they wanted to chastise her.

'Why aren't you in Mallorca?' she moaned, filling the kettle with water and flicking it on.

'I don't want a hot drink.'

'Well, I do.'

Lauren peered at Magnolia rather too closely before frowning. 'What's wrong with your face?'

'What do you mean?'

'Your skin has a strange, silvery sheen.'

'Oh, that. I ran out of proper face moisturiser because I haven't been out, so I had to use body moisturiser instead.'

'Oh, Magnolia! You need to look after yourself.'

'It's only moisturiser. Give me a break.'

'You've had a break. Magnolia — please don't tell me you've given up your chocolate shop just because of that nasty little nitwit.'

'Mum, he trashed the place!'

156

'He threw a few chocolates and bottles of booze on the floor — and then ran away. He didn't set the place alight, or anything.'

Yeah, only because Patricia scared him off before it escalated any further, Magnolia thought grimly. She rubbed her eyes and shakily spooned coffee into the cafetiere. 'What Mathias did was just the final straw,' she said quietly. 'It's too difficult. I need to be in a calm state of mind to make chocolate, but my head's too crammed full of all the other stuff I need to do to make the business a success.'

She poured hot water onto the coffee and joined her mother at the kitchen table, leaving it to brew. 'The waitressing job is only temporary,' she insisted to her mother. 'Not that there's anything wrong with waitressing for a living. I admire people who do it. But I'm only doing it until I find another office administration job.'

She tried to ignore the flutter of panic she felt in her chest, that phantom squeeze around her throat after saying this, which had become an almost daily occurrence in the time leading up to her purchase of the shop.

I'm trapped, I'm trapped, I'm trapped.

Lauren's lips pursed to one side, her eyes moving in the opposite direction, as though something had just occurred to her. Magnolia knew the look.

'What, Mum?'

'I'm just thinking... maybe Mathias wants you back. Maybe making a fuss in the shop was his way of trying to grab your attention. Perhaps he wanted to make a grand, masculine gesture and he just... went about it in the wrong way.'

'Wow. How did you come up with that one?' Magnolia threw her head back and laughed deeply, the front legs of her chair lifting off the floor, before she realised and quickly resettled them.

'It's possible.'

'Yeah, maybe he wants us to get back together so that he can persuade me to open a gaming lounge instead of a chocolate shop. He could fill it with ugly chairs and humongous screens... he could fit blackout blinds on all the windows... probably put a beer keg or two in the corner.

'Mum, I'm absolutely sure that he doesn't want me back. Neither of us really wanted each other in the first place. We only ended up together because of circumstance and convenience. We had nothing in common whatsoever.'

'It was only a hypothesis. I don't actually want you to get back together with him; despite the fact that you're not getting any younger and it worries me that you're not with someone, please give me some credit.'

'I don't need to be with someone right now.'

'If you were, they'd be able to support you through this bump in the road.'

'Oh, whatever. You're hurting my head.' As if to emphasise the fact, Magnolia crossed her arms on the kitchen table, letting her head drop into the crook they formed. She could hear her mother's perfect nails tapping slowly and rhythmically on the table. She lifted her head a little to see what colour they were today — oyster pink.

Recovering, she lifted her head completely and set about pouring coffee for both of them, despite Lauren's earlier protestation that she didn't want one.

'What are those awful things on your feet?'

Magnolia looked down in alarm, expecting that something unwelcome had occurred. It hadn't. 'They're slipper boots.'

'They make a terrible shuffling noise when you walk around.'

'Well, you don't have to be here to suffer through it, do you? I didn't invite you round. 'Anyway — enough about that; why are you here? Why aren't you in Mallorca?'

'We decided to sell the house. The Fitzgeralds moved out, but rather than rent it to new people, we thought we'd spruce it up a bit, sell it, and use the money to buy an apartment for when we come back to visit. I think Mark and Claire are getting a bit weary of us staying at their place every time, and those new apartments overlooking the river are rather spectacular. Seeing as we were coming home for Christmas this year anyway, we thought we'd extend the visit to get the

159

house sorted. And a jolly good thing we did, too, seeing the mess you're making of your life. Don't think I didn't notice you changing the subject.'

Magnolia rolled her eyes and sipped her coffee.

'Right — this is what we're going to do: you're going to quit that waitressing job and give yourself a couple of weeks off to recharge your batteries; I'm going to make the finishing touches to the decor in the shop, and knock up a few batches of long-life chocolate products that can be made now, ready for the shop opening. Claire gave me your spare key, so I'll get things going again, and when you're ready to come back—'

'Oh my God, Mum, no!' Magnolia's jaw dropped. Her fingers, which had been wrapped around her mug, jolted in shock, sending coffee sloshing onto the table.

'What? If I can caramelise carrots for my legendary Sunday roasts, I'm sure I can caramelise some almonds and douse them in chocolate. Easy-peasy. And I'm sure I saw some tins of salmon-pink paint when I was over at the house earlier, leftover from when we did the bathroom. It'll look great on the shop walls. First of all, I'll—'

'There's absolutely no way in this world!'

Magnolia forcefully pushed away from the table and stood, hands on hips, glaring at her mother, who was a picture of wide-eyed innocence. She then snatched the dishcloth from the draining board and began attacking the coffee spillage.

'I'll go back tomorrow,' she snapped. '*On my own.* I don't want you interfering — you haven't got a clue.'

'Marvellous.' Lauren's eyes gleamed in triumphant amusement as she snapped her butter-cream leather gloves back on and rose elegantly from the table. As they walked together to the front door, she inclined her head at the letter regarding Agnes' will, on the console table. 'Oh, and that was a gift from a wonderful woman whose dying wish was that you use it to help make your dreams of opening Cocomolioco a reality. Make sure you use it.'

Suddenly sheepish and thoughtful, Magnolia nodded in capitulation. She opened her arms to embrace her mother; she still smelt of mimosa, a scent she'd been wearing since Magnolia's childhood. 'How are you getting back?' she asked, looking down at Lauren's stilettos.

'Mark's outside in the car.'

'Oh, right.'

Magnolia waved at her brother from the open doorway, drawing her fleecy dressing-gown close, as Lauren sashayed to the car.

'Done,' Lauren declared to her son, shutting the car door.

Mark raised his eyebrows. 'How did you manage that? Claire and I have been trying all sorts of ways to reason with her over the last few days.'

'Easy-peasy. There's the right way, the wrong way — and a mother's way.'

Mark wasn't impressed. 'I reckon you just wore her down by instilling a deadly combination of confusion, frustration and fear that you were going to take over.'

'Yes, like I said — a mother's way.'

Lauren flipped down the sun visor, swished free the enclosed mirror, and checked her lipstick. 'Now... shall we go to the fishmongers? I feel like cooking black cod for dinner.'

Chapter Seventeen

'Oh, for Christ's sake, Patricia!' Magnolia yelled, as she unlocked the shop door the next morning, taking a step forward, before immediately stepping backwards again in fright. Two teenage boys walking past, trying to stuff bacon sandwiches into their mouths as quickly as possible, sprayed meat and bread onto the pavement as they laughed at her reaction.

Patricia, who had been looming in a sinister manner just behind the door, commanding a wooden chopping board to float in the air above the threshold — thankfully out of sight of the boys — relaxed and stood down. 'You're back!' she exclaimed joyfully.

'And what a wonderful welcome,' Magnolia responded sarcastically, quickly entering and closing the door. 'Why were you crouching in the shadows, waiting to bash me on the head? I'm very grateful that you did it to Mathias, but I didn't expect it to become a regular habit.'

'You've been gone for days! Suspicious people started hanging around and peering through the windows. I didn't know what was happening.'

'What suspicious people?'

'A woman with bright green eyes — like yours, but with a more inquisitive look in them, and far too much eyeliner; she was wearing a fedora and had really knobbly knuckles.'

'How old was she?'

'I'd say a well-preserved fifty-five.'

'That'll be my mum.'

'She's a bit nosy, isn't she? What's she up to?'

Magnolia sighed. 'She's just worried about me.'

'Oh, I've finally seen Jed!' Patricia remembered, enthusiastically. 'He was one of those peering through the window. I guess he wondered why everything was so quiet. He has lovely eyes. They're almost violet. Back in the day, I had a china doll I was trying to sell with exactly the same eye colour.'

'Don't tell me... it's in the outbuilding.'

'No — I crushed it, that night. It was on display, and in my line of destruction. Nathan will have cleared it away with all the other detritus.'

Well, that brought the mood down. 'Sorry,' Magnolia winced.

Patricia shrugged in acceptance. 'It's OK.'

'How did you know it was Jed, anyway?'

'Because he splayed his hands on the windowpane and they were covered in massive globs of dough.'

Magnolia's head snapped towards Patricia in surprise.

'Oh, don't be so ridiculously gullible! Of course he didn't!' Patricia gave a great cackle. 'A discombobulated young lady in an apron came rushing over to him shouting "Jed! A customer wants to know what *fougasse* is." Apparently, as I discovered there and then, it's speciality bread from Provence.'

'Good to know you've had some entertainment and education whilst I've been away.'

'Who's the dishy guy with salt-and-pepper hair and a cinematic, brooding demeanour?'

'Who?'

'That's what I'm asking you. Anyway, he was here yesterday, but he's also here right now.' Patricia cocked her head at the door.

'Oh, that's my dad!' Magnolia threw the door open. 'Escaping from Mum already?'

Joe stepped into the shop, looking around with evident approval. 'I couldn't really see what you'd done to the place from outside… it looks great.'

'Thanks.'

'Anyway, don't be cheeky. I wanted to make sure you really were coming back. How are you?'

'Fine thanks, Dad.'

He looked at her seriously. 'It's a real question, Nolly.'

'Honestly, I'm fine. I had a bit of a wobble, but I'm OK now. It's not supposed to be easy, is it? But it should be fun… and it was, until recently. I'm working my way back towards that.'

'You should have reported that bastard to the police.'

Magnolia shrugged. 'No point. He won't be back — I scared him off.'

'How'd you manage that?' Joe looked dubious.

'I hit him over the head with a stoneware bowl. *He* could report *me*. He won't though, I'm sure. That's the end of it.'

'OK — whatever you think.' Joe wandered over to one of the gauges on the shelf brackets and tapped it, as though expecting something to happen.

'Why are you doing that?' Magnolia asked. 'It's not connected to anything. It's not going to read your fortune or anything fantastical like that.'

'Just curious,' he replied easily. He sank onto a stool, placing a mystery box he'd brought along with him on the adjacent stool. 'I've brought you a top hat. I wondered if I could swap it for a piece of cake, or something.'

'That's an unusual swap suggestion.'

'I thought it would fit with your steampunk theme. You could try to find some of those aviator goggles to go with it and use it upended to hold little bags of chocolate. I just thought it'd be something a bit different, rather than having everything regimentally displayed on the shelves, perhaps.'

He opened what was now apparently a hat box and retrieved the top hat — a luxuriously glossy midnight-blue silk one — with a flourish.

'Wow, it's marvellous!' Magnolia reached out for it eagerly, turning it around with curiosity when Joe handed it over. 'Where did you get it from?'

'Your mum bought me it for Mark and Claire's wedding. God knows what she was thinking. Obviously, I didn't wear it — it didn't fit with the overall bohemian look they were going for. And I don't even suit top hats. So it's never been worn. You can put stuff in it without worrying it'll be all sweaty.'

Magnolia laughed. 'OK, good to know.' She flipped it upside down, positioned it on a shelf, and stood back to take in the effect. 'Ooo, it definitely will look great with chocolates in it, Dad. Thanks!'

'How about finding some cake for me, then?'

'You know I hardly ever make cakes. You'll have to be content with chocolate. I've got some dark chocolate with cranberry and cinnamon crisp, if you'd like that?'

'Yeah, that sounds good. Can you give me enough to see me through a forty-mile bike ride?'

'You're worse than Mark!' Magnolia called over her shoulder, as she went into the kitchen for the requested chocolate. She returned with a generously-sized greaseproof paper-wrapped bundle, which Joe gleefully deposited in the not-long-empty hatbox.

'What are you up to today, then? Do you need a hand with anything?'

'No, thanks. I'm going to varnish the floor. That's what I was trying to do last week before Mathias distracted me in rather spectacular fashion.'

'OK. What are these for?' Joe gestured towards two desk lamps on the hot chocolate counter. 'They don't seem your usual style.'

'Oh, yeah — you can help me with that, actually, before you go.' Magnolia walked over and switched both lamps on. 'They're for test purposes. Which light bulb will be best for my chandeliers? Do you think the yellow — for a warm, gentle glow; or the white — for a cool, crisp illumination?'

'Definitely the yellow,' Joe said firmly. 'You want a vintage effect, don't you?'

'Absolutely; thanks, Dad.'

'Well, on that note, I'll be off. I'm happy to be of service.'

'I definitely think he'd suit a top hat. Very suave,' Patricia declared dreamily, as Joe departed.

Magnolia looked around to make sure he'd gone. 'Don't you be lusting after my dad,' she said firmly, wagging her finger in mock admonishment.

'Oh, give me a break — I have so little joy left.'

Magnolia's gaze suddenly became serious. 'I missed you, you know?' She moved towards Patricia as if she was going to embrace her, before she remembered the futility of the attempt. 'I came back to pick up my dreams, and because Agnes believed I could do it, but I also came back because I missed spending time with you.'

Patricia shook her head regretfully. 'Magnolia, dear, you mustn't make decisions based on an assumption of my ongoing presence. I *am* going to move on — and soon — I just don't know exactly when.'

Magnolia gave a weak smile. 'OK. But at this moment, it's good to see you again. I'm going to get on with varnishing the floor. Are you going to stick around?'

'Do you have another brush? Can I help?'

Magnolia shrugged her shoulders. 'Sure. If you think you can manage the pressure and motion?'

Apparently, she couldn't.

Patricia's brush, whilst dipping into the varnish cleanly enough, scuttled disconcertingly and creepily across the floor like a huge spider.

'OK, you'd better stop,' Magnolia declared after about five minutes, snatching Patricia's brush then visibly shuddering. 'It's starting to creep me out.'

Patricia sighed. 'OK. It's boring, anyway. I'm going to the outbuilding for a while. Will you make me a hot chocolate to take with me?'

Magnolia got to her feet to make two hot chocolates — one destined never to be drunk but prized nevertheless for its scent — and then returned her attention to the floor.

She couldn't concentrate, though. Well, not concentrate… rather, go with the flow. She could still see Patricia from the corner of her eye. She put the varnish brush down and leaned back on her heels. 'Why are you loitering with intent?'

'Hmpfh!' Patricia zoomed forward, somewhat affronted. Her mug of hot chocolate bobbed on the air alongside her before settling on the hot chocolate counter with a little dip, spilling a little of the foamy top.

'Your father has rather stolen my thunder.'

'My father? You mean Dad?'

'It's the same thing.'

'Yes, but when you say "father" it's like he's a vicar, or something. Why has he stolen your thunder, anyway? You were going all gooey over him not so long ago. Now you want to stamp on his head.'

'Magnolia, I didn't say that I wanted to stamp on his head!'

Magnolia rolled her eyes. 'Tell me why he's stolen your thunder.'

'Can you open the outbuilding door and back kitchen door, please?'

'Why?'

'I have a *coco de mer* for you, and although I can levitate it, I can't seem to transport it through closed doors in the same way that I can transport myself.'

'You have a *what?* Never mind, just show me.'

Magnolia duly opened the two doors, and before long, a brown object the size and shape of a woman's buttocks floated forth, under the control of Patricia's paranormal gaze.

'What's that?'

'I told you. It's a *coco de mer*, a sea coconut; the seed pod of a special palm tree found in the Seychelles. They fall into the sea and gradually, over time, the husk erodes and leaves this lovely polished inner nut. They appear on the shore, washed up with the tide.'

'Oh, right. For a moment there, I thought you were going to pretend it was a cocoa bean.'

Patricia huffed indignantly through her nose and planted her hands on her hips. 'Charming! I just thought you might want it as an unusual decorative item in the shop. I was just about to present it to you when your dad walked in and stole my thunder by giving you something as well. They're quite rare, you know. Rarer than your dad's top hat, that's for sure.'

'Why is it shaped like a pair of buttocks?'

'They're two-lobed; double coconuts. They're supposed to look like that.'

'Let me think about it for a while. It is rather interesting, and I appreciate you thinking of me, but I'm not sure yet whether I'll have the space, once all my products are here. If I could display chocolates in or on it, it would be a different matter, of course.'

Patricia's lips pursed.

'I'm not saying Dad's top hat was better... just more practical as an addition to the shop. Your *coco de*

171

mer is definitely more intriguing. I just need to think how to use it.'

That seemed to pacify her. Magnolia sighed with relief and commenced with the varnishing.

'I'm going to visit my moor,' Patricia announced. 'My imagination is particularly vibrant at the moment. I think I'll even be able to visualise some cheese and biscuits with a glass of port.'

'The school kids are on their lunch break, so they'll probably drown out the sound of your burbling brook,' Magnolia warned. On a trip to the local garden centre with Claire, she'd bought a small water feature to enhance Patricia's moorland experience.

Patricia shrugged, unperturbed. 'I'll just pretend they're woodland elves.'

A glob of varnish fell from Magnolia's brush and she quickly spread it out on the floor before it had a chance to dry lumpy.

Chapter Eighteen

It was market day in the town centre, and Magnolia arrived at the shop feeling rather flustered and distracted by all the extra activity along her usually smooth route. Patricia appeared immediately, trying to command her attention before she'd even set down her bags.

'There's a strange man with a load of gear, around the back,' she declared.

'I know. It'll be Alex. I thought I'd be here earlier to meet him. He's here to paint the starry night's sky on the ceiling.'

'Oh, wonderful; so, I'll be imprisoned in the outbuilding all day, then,' Patricia huffed. 'I'm guessing you won't want me in here, complicating your social interactions.'

'You like it in there!'

'I only like to be in there when it suits me.'

'I'll bring the radio through for you. As long as you promise not to have the volume turned up too high.'

'OK. I want a hot chocolate too, though.'

Magnolia glugged from her water bottle, slicked on some lip balm, and rushed past Patricia to greet Alex in the garden. Once she'd brought him through to the shop, then she'd transfer the radio. Otherwise, if he noticed her doing it, he'd think it was a bit weird.

Incredibly, the starry night's sky was painted within the day. Magnolia helped to paint the base colour, whilst Alex concentrated on the stars and extra definition. She was so pleased with the result, that as well as paying him the agreed fee, she also offered to make some truffles for his sister's upcoming fortieth birthday party.

She hadn't realised until now that the place had been missing a certain magic. The ceiling looked truly remarkable. It featured the most prominent constellations, in roughly the right place, against a night sky the same midnight blue colour as Magnolia's brand identity palette and hence the shop signage. Here and there, the suggestion of a little cloud cover added a mysterious smokiness. In contrast with the creamy, plain walls, Magnolia thought it made the shop seem to be floating roofless in time and space.

'I hope it doesn't give your customers vertigo,' Patricia said darkly. 'They might end up knocking all your chocolates off the shelves by accident. You could be spending all your time tidying up after them.'

'Oh, Patricia! I'll take my chances.' Magnolia gave a joyful twirl across the floor.

After a long day of decorating, then a short day of cleaning and organising, it was back to chocolate making.

'I need to atone for my sins.'

Melting chocolate at the hob for dipping Florentines, Magnolia looked down at herself. 'I don't seem to be wearing my dog collar today.'

'Don't be like that.' Patricia sidled over. 'Those poor people I terrorised. The people who had the pizza takeaway, and the shoe business before that. What if I ruined their businesses beyond recovery? What if they're destitute because of me?'

'What if they are? How do you propose to fix it?'

'I could give them money. Well... I could let you know how to access my money — I do have quite a lot of savings — and you could somehow give a chunk of it to them. You could just post it to them. They don't need to know where it's come from.'

'Like some sort of weird Father Christmas?'

'I suppose.'

'That's all very noble of you, but you're forgetting a key detail. You don't have money anymore, remember. You're dead. It's gone to whoever you left it to in your will, whether that be Nathan, or whoever. And if you didn't have a will, I guess it's gone to Nathan anyway.'

'Oh, no!' Patricia was dismayed. 'It's not that I don't want Nathan to have it — of course I do — it just would have been nice to give something to those poor people.'

Magnolia switched the hob off and poured the bowlful of melted dark chocolate onto the cold marble worktop. She then swirled it around with a palette knife, spreading it thin and then gathering the outermost edges back into the centre as Patricia had now seen her do many times, cooling it down quickly and evenly as necessary. Patricia stood by her elbow, joyfully taking in the scent.

'Please can you move back a bit? You're distracting me.'

'Oh, we'll talk about it next month, or the month after that instead, shall we?' Patricia huffed. 'It's not as though I have a life or anywhere to go.'

'No, it's fine — we can discuss it now. I'm only dipping Florentines for a couple of upcoming birthdays. I'm not doing anything fiddly.' Patricia looked pacified. Magnolia reached for the Florentines.

'I wouldn't worry too much about those poor people,' Magnolia placated her. 'My brother knows Luca, the owner of Pizza Pizzazz. They were going to move on from here anyway — it was too small for them. They wanted to have a proper restaurant. Now they have *two* restaurants in the area — they're really successful. As for the couple who had the shoe business — they're both in prison. They moved on to another unit from here, but then they were done for fraud and people trafficking.'

'Oh, right,' Patricia looked taken aback. 'That's that, then.'

Magnolia looked up from the Florentines. She knew Patricia was by no means finished, and merely

176

contemplating something, by the tell-tale tilt of her head to one side.

'Actually, now that you mention it, the staff were always darting around nervously with a cornered look in their eyes.'

'Yeah, that's what happens when a ghost terrorises you.'

'I didn't terrorise the staff! I only terrorised the business owners — before and after the staff had gone for the day.'

'Well, they'll have still heard spooky stories about you from the owners, won't they?'

'They were committing fraud and people trafficking — how awful! I should have caused even more of a hullabaloo than I did. I was too busy concentrating on levitating heavy objects and making maximum noise to notice their shady dealings. Though I did notice that the shoes they sold were very poor quality. They'd have a selection on display in the shop window, and the dye would fade from the so-called leather within just a few days.'

'So says the woman who made her fortune buying *papier mache* eggs from primary school summer fetes and selling them on as Fabergé.'

'I never did that! Who said I did that?'

Magnolia knew she shouldn't tease Patricia so much, but it was difficult to resist, when she was on the receiving end of it from her so often. Besides, it was funny. She softened. 'Look, you're making up for it now, aren't you? You might have scared off the previous tenants, but you didn't do anything that led to anyone's downfall. And now you're helping me to become a success. So the scales of goodness are tipped in your favour.'

'Maybe,' Patricia murmured.

'Don't go,' Magnolia implored, as she made to slink away. 'I'm working on the content for my website after I've finished with this, and it'd be great if you could help me.'

'Help you with what, exactly?'

'The design. Come on, I'll make a fresh hot chocolate, too.'

'You've still got that one.'

'I know, but it's stopped steaming, and I know you can't smell it when the steam goes away.'

Chapter Nineteen

On the day that Magnolia was experimenting with different hot chocolate toppings, something extraordinary happened. Having thought the discovery of a ghost in her fledgling chocolate shop was the most extraordinary thing that had, and ever would, happen to her, for something else extraordinary to happen in quick succession was certainly saying something.

Patricia had been roped in to help decide which toppings were the best, and at one end, the curved marble slab that comprised the hot chocolate counter was covered with various apparatus and ingredients, with six steaming earthenware mugs of hot chocolate neatly lined up at the other end.

'I don't know!' Patricia cried, aghast. 'How would I know? I can't taste the damn stuff. Surely, you've got a friend with taste buds who can help you instead?'

Magnolia rolled her eyes in exasperation. 'I've already told you. At this stage I just need to know which three *look* the best.'

There was a pause. Patricia's eyes flitted between the six mugs. She took a step closer and studied them more carefully. They were all topped with a luxurious swirl of whipped cream, but different finishing flourishes.

'Don't take too long about it though,' said Magnolia, waving a spatula around. 'Everything'll melt or deflate, and it'll be too late to make a proper judgement.'

'Those three,' Patricia said, suddenly decisive; she pointed at one with sugared rose petals and pistachio dust, one with sugared violet petals and blueberry dust, and one with delicate zigzags of caramel. Magnolia was thrilled — it was the exact three she'd been hoping she'd choose.

'Great! I knew you had a good eye for design behind that dodgy, antiques dealing façade!' she exclaimed, with an injection of warmth to temper the insult.

Just then, the door opened. And the *something extraordinary* happened.

A man stepped over the threshold.

'Sorry... the door was ajar,' he said, somewhat embarrassed. His voice sounded raspy, as though he was unaccustomed to using it lately. Magnolia was vaguely aware of a pool of hot chocolate seeping into the long sleeve of her fussy broderie-anglaise blouse. She wondered why the *Closed* sign hadn't deterred him regardless, and then noticed it had blown to the floor.

'Um, that's OK,' she replied. 'Is there something I can help you with?'

He stood uncomfortably in the doorway. 'Well…
the thing is…'

'It's Nathan!' Patricia hissed over her shoulder, at
the exact moment he finished with:

'I used to own this shop. I was just being nosy, I
suppose.'

Magnolia felt five emotions simultaneously:
elation on behalf of Patricia, that her son had finally
come back; joy that she could invite this gorgeous man
in and entice him with hot chocolate without worrying
if he was a psychopath; intrigue that this gorgeous man
was actually Patricia's son; panic over how she was
going to be able to strike up a conversation with him
that somehow led to addressing the ghostly presence of
his mother, and thereafter hopefully facilitated her
crossover to the other side; and curiosity as to whether
he could actually see Patricia now, as Magnolia could.
She was his mother, after all, if that made a difference.

Patricia began zipping up and down the shop with
frenzied emotion, scurrying across not only the floor but
the walls as well. The fact that Nathan maintained an
awkward yet calm demeanour throughout this led
Magnolia to quickly conclude that he hadn't developed
an ability to see her since his last visit to the shop.

'I guess the place looks quite different,' she said
brightly and rather nervously. 'Come in, if you'd like to.
The shop's not officially open yet, I'm just using the
kitchen to trial a few things, but if you like hot chocolate

there's six going spare. Actually... make that five... I seem to have knocked one over.'

'That'd be great. Thanks.' He stepped tentatively forward, taking in the décor with apparent appreciation, before pulling loose one of the stools at the chocolate bar. Crouching down for a closer look at the iron base before sitting, he gave a faint whistle of wonder at the footrest, which was formed from the pedals of a vintage bicycle; the chain and cog had also been retained and gloriously upcycled.

'The perks of having a brother who owns a cycling shop,' Magnolia said, noticing his close attention to the detail, as he then stroked the cherry-red leather seat pad before finally sitting.

'The whole place looks incredible! I'm so glad it's you who has it now. I mean... you've really brought a touch of magic. It's just what's needed around here.'

Magnolia gave an embarrassed laugh. 'You haven't even tried the produce, yet.'

He gazed with a mix of anticipation and indecision at the five mugs of hot chocolate laid out before him. 'You can try all of them, if you like — but that one's probably the best.' She pointed to the one with the sugared violet petals and blueberry dust.

He rather dramatically grasped the mug with one hand then wrapped both hands around it as though it was the elixir of life. He was wearing a long-sleeved T-shirt rolled to his elbows, and Magnolia couldn't help noticing he had great forearms, toned and well-shaped.

She'd been attracted to him from the moment she saw him, but was trying to avoid looking at him directly; not so much in an attempt to play it cool, but under some ridiculous notion that if she didn't look at him properly, he likewise wouldn't look at her properly. Her hair needed washing, and she reckoned her face looked pinched and haggard after too many late nights, too many glasses of wine, and not enough time outside in the fresh air.

His hair, however, was glorious. It fell to his chin in loose waves — delightfully unruly, with wild streaks of silver running through the dark brown. He clearly didn't believe in taming it the way Patricia did hers. He had a strong jawline and his eyes were a green-brown, gold-flecked wonder.

'This is delicious.' He gazed intently at his hot chocolate for a couple of seconds, as if he might discover its secret by doing so.

'Thanks. It took a while to get right,' Magnolia replied modestly. She flailed around, trying to think of a question which wasn't likely to be as inflammatory as *"Why did you close your antiques shop?"*

'I've been away for a while, so I didn't know what had become of this place,' Nathan said, rescuing her from her internal struggle.

'Working abroad, or something?'

'Not primarily. I was travelling around France and Italy for a few months, mainly for... I was soul-searching and looking for inspiration, I suppose. That sounds so lame and self-obsessed, doesn't it? I did do a bit of bar work out there as well though, to keep my finances healthy. Does that sound better?'

'That's better. You're not really bourgeois, then' Magnolia responded, with a cheeky smile.

'Oh, I have an impressive list of character failings worse than bourgeois,' he responded, deadpan. They eyed each other and both chuckled. Magnolia had completely forgotten about Patricia's presence, which was just as well really, as her slack-jawed astonishment would have been rather distracting.

Nathan checked the time on his watch — not his phone, how refreshing — and extended his lean yet muscular frame from the stool. 'Damn, I need to go. How much do I owe you for the hot chocolate?'

'Oh, don't be daft. You were my test case. You were doing me a favour — market research and all that.'

'Well thank you. It really was extraordinarily good.'

They stood looking at each other for an inordinate amount of time. Magnolia finally broke the spell by fussing with the chocolate-stained cuff of her blouse.

'I have a vintage brass and copper diving helmet that would look great in here, if you want it?' Nathan offered. 'One of many leftovers from the antiques business we used to have. It would make me feel better about not paying for the hot chocolate if you were to give it a good home.'

'That would be amazing, thanks!'

Magnolia accompanied Nathan to the shop door.

'So... I'll drop by with the diving helmet within the next few days?' he suggested.

'Great... can you phone or text first though?' she asked. *God, that sounded so unfriendly.* 'It's just that... I'm usually here... but the shop door's not usually open. Most of the time I'm faffing about with melted chocolate in the kitchen and it can be a bit frantic... I can't always stop in the middle of making something, because the temperatures have to be carefully controlled.' *Great — now I seem not only unfriendly but also self-important — as though I'm conducting brain surgery or cultivating organisms for the next big drug to combat a killer disease.*

Unperturbed, Nathan just smiled easily and retrieved his phone. 'Sure, what's your number?' he asked. Then he paused, phone outstretched in his hand, forgotten, to look at her in astonishment.

'Wow, can you believe we nearly forgot to exchange names?'

Well, it's more understandable that I'd forget — seeing as I already know your *name*, Magnolia thought wryly. 'Magnolia,' she responded with a smile, almost reaching out for a handshake, before deciding it would add a note of formality that had been delightfully absent from their encounter thus far. She twiddled with her earlobe instead.

'Magnolia — and to think I nearly didn't know,' he said, reaching for her hand anyway. He took it in his as if he was about to ask her to dance, and then blew a kiss from afar at her knuckles in some wondrous, witty approximation of the antiquated way a gentleman used to address a lady.

'I'm Nathan,' he said.

'Why didn't you make a noise to draw his attention?' Magnolia asked incredulously, once Nathan had departed. Patricia sighed and plopped down from the newly installed glass counter where she'd been sitting. 'And you shouldn't be sitting on there, by, the way.'

'Why? It's not as though I have any weight anymore to break it.'

'If you don't have any weight, then you don't need to sit down to rest. There's no gravity effect on you. Anyway, I'm sure it's still unhygienic. I need to display my "choose your own selection" chocolates in there soon, and I don't want you getting in the habit of sitting on it.'

'Unhygienic ghosts!' Patricia cackled. 'Now I've heard it all.'

'So why didn't you draw Nathan's attention somehow? I know you have more in your repertoire than what you unleashed on Mathias… you could have used some sort of more gentle and subtle poltergeist approach.'

'Of course I could have. But it's too soon.'

'*It's too soon?* This is what you've been waiting for! Your whole reason for still being here!'

'It's too soon,' Patricia repeated firmly. She slunk away to the outbuilding.

Magnolia brought her hand to her forehead in disbelief.

Chapter Twenty

Late summer drifting into early autumn was Magnolia's favourite time of year. The searing white light of high summer changed to a honeyed glow that somehow warmed her soul more; the glow itself seeming to carry a scent — of hot, buttered toast and caramelised nuts.

'What do you think?' she asked, stepping back from the mirror she was decorating with old cogs and gears. She wasn't at the glue gun stage yet — the mirror was laid horizontally on the hot chocolate counter, and she was using tape and a pencil to outline roughly where she wanted each part to be positioned.

Patricia screwed up her face. 'It's a bit odd. Why do you want to ruin a perfectly fine frame with all that clunky nonsense?'

'Because it's boring otherwise! I thought you liked what I was doing?'

Patricia shrugged, non-committal, as Magnolia sank down onto a bar stool, deflated. She then looked back up at her, quizzically.

'Why are you looking at me like that?'

'I was just wondering... why aren't you wearing one of those awful hospital gowns? Y'know... you died

188

in hospital, so as a ghost, shouldn't you be wearing whatever clothing you died in?'

'Oh, I never thought. I don't know. Thank heavens that's not the case though! Although I would have liked to have been wearing the antique cameo brooch that Nathan bought me for my sixtieth birthday as well. I wonder who decided it'd be this,' Patricia mused, looking down at herself.

'So you and Nathan were close at one time, then, despite the way that it ended?'

'Oh yes. It was only in the last couple of years that it all turned bad; when he became involved with the business. It was clear within the first few weeks that we had our little differences about what sales approach to take — which should have served as a warning.'

'Why did you go into business together in the first place? Or, more importantly, why did you stay in business together if it was so fractious?'

'Well, in hindsight we obviously shouldn't have.' Patricia sighed, looking contemplative. 'It's not what Nathan wanted to do with his life, anyway. He studied English at university. He wanted to be a writer. It was his father and I who set up the antiques business before Nathan was born.

'Nathan was a copywriter for an advertising agency. He was happy enough there, but he was made redundant. So, he gave himself a year off to write a novel; if he was unsuccessful in making a career out of that, he was going to look for another copywriting job.

But then Eric — that's Nathan's father — who'd been a raging alcoholic for some years by then, went and died on us. I can see now that Nathan only came into the business when Eric died in an attempt to support me. I should have just retired, but I was scared to. I didn't know what to do instead. Of course, now I can think of a hundred and one things I wish I'd done.

'I wish I'd experienced the rich sensory overload of the markets in Marrakesh. I wish I'd had a Singapore sling in the Raffles Hotel. I'd have loved to have planted a rose garden and grown globe artichokes. I could have sat amongst my roses, eating my globe artichokes; pulling the petals off one by one and dipping them into melted lemon butter.'

Magnolia just smiled at her sympathetically. Patricia now had a blissful, faraway look on her face, and she didn't want to interrupt it with empty platitudes.

'Did you love him?' she finally asked softly. 'Eric, I mean.'

'Yes — in the beginning. Or did I? I'm beginning to wonder, now. Sorry, I know that sounds ridiculously inconclusive. It's just that I spent so many years *not* loving him, that the initial few years of loving him seem as insubstantial as a faded dream.

'How do you know whether you stopped loving someone because they changed into another person, or whether they were never the original person you loved, anyway? How do you know that the original person wasn't just an illusion brought about by your own projections and fantasies?'

'I've never loved anyone,' Magnolia admitted, embarrassed, 'Even though I'm in my mid-thirties. In a romantic way, I mean. I've never been *in* love, as they say.' Patricia didn't seem surprised to hear this; during their time together at the shop, she'd obviously picked up on more than Magnolia had realised. 'But I do know what you mean about a relationship being an illusion brought about by your own projections and fantasies.'

They both contemplated this for a moment.

'How did Eric and Nathan get along with each other?' Magnolia finally asked. Patricia sighed and became even more maudlin.

'Their relationship was characterised by indifference. It got to the point where they didn't care enough to even argue with each other. There was a prevailing sense of ennui whenever they were in the same room.

'Eric was a functioning alcoholic by day, an incoherent idiot by night; it began when Nathan was about five years old. He was highly successful in the antiques industry — he had an eye for the gems and the patter to make a cracking good deal. But after a great day's work, come the early evening, he was so far gone on wine and then whisky that he couldn't even read Nathan a bedtime story. It was heart-breaking to watch Nathan imploring him to read something; it was even worse when he agreed, but couldn't even string a sentence together, or rambled off on a crazy tangent. Worst of all though was when eventually Nathan completely gave up on asking him.

'Then there was one terrible day when he turned up drunk to one of Nathan's school football matches. It wasn't enough for him to yell abuse from the sidelines, either — he actually broke onto the pitch and started tackling the players. If it hadn't been for his alcohol-induced shocking lack of coordination, he could have caused one of those kids an injury; they were only nine years old. The other parents were appalled and Nathan's school mates thought it was a pathetic display. It took poor Nathan months to get over the embarrassment. That was the day that any hope of them ever having a close father-son bond really shattered.'

Patricia's image turned a subdued grey-blue putty colour; it was only at that moment that Magnolia realised that her form was usually edged in silver, which was absent now, as it had been when she first told Magnolia about the reason she believed she was still here — and also when Magnolia had failed to find Nathan at his house.

Patricia continued.

'He died of liver psoriasis not long after his sixty-second birthday. I did feel a sense of loss — for what might have been, rather than for what we actually had together by the end; loss with a vein of relief running through it. It was relief not only for me, but also for Nathan. Eric would never have made up for being a disappointing father... at least with his death Nathan wouldn't have continuous fresh validation from his daily behaviour.'

'I can see how it was an emotionally confusing time for you both,' Magnolia said softly. She wished she could hug Patricia. It seemed so unnatural that she couldn't hug her; which was testimony to just how human her friend still was, even as a ghost, to engender these feelings.

'Where did you meet Eric?' Magnolia asked. She changed her cross-legged position to the opposite side; she'd stopped decorating the mirror and was now sitting on a bar stool whilst listening to Patricia. The sheet she'd laid under the mirror to protect the counter from glue and scratches caught her leg and dragged loose, so she quickly re-positioned it.

'My dad was an auctioneer,' Patricia replied, as she smiled at more pleasant memories. 'He specialised in vintage toys: train sets, porcelain dolls, teddy bears, elaborate dolls' houses and that that kind of thing. When I was a teenager, I used to love helping out with the displays at the auction house.

'I was nineteen when Eric first made an appearance; he had a vast collection of clockwork toys to sell, though I can't remember where he got them from. He was told to bring them to me for displaying. I was immediately smitten — he looked and dressed like Mick Jagger. All the other boys around me at that time were trying to be like The Beatles or Simon and

Garfunkel, and it was quite wearisome. He had an edgy yet calm way about him — and, wow, he did make me laugh. He had such a sarcastic sense of humour.

'After that first visit to the auction house, he came back another three times before he asked me out on a date. We went to a restaurant and had fondue — it was all the rage back then. I felt so sophisticated! Well, I did until what felt like a kilo of cheese descended into my stomach and sat there like a rock.

'The first date ended rather chastely, but after another couple of outings at the cinema, we went back to the flat he shared with friends and listened to The Rolling Stones on his record player until we ended up in bed. It was the *Let it Bleed* album; we must have played *You Can't Always Get What You Want* about five times that night.'

Magnolia smiled at Patricia affectionately. A couple of months ago she'd only had a vague notion of The Rolling Stones; now, thanks to Patricia, she knew most of their back catalogue — they were still going, apparently — and had even found herself dipping and swirling chocolate in time with the rhythm of their songs, whilst Patricia joyfully strutted in the background in the manner of Mick.

Twice now, Mark had called round whilst Magnolia had the radio tuned to Patricia's favourite station. He was certainly curious and rather amused by this new development, though he didn't seem to dwell on the reason for her sudden interest in the music that was popular before her birth.

'I suppose it was music and art that kept us together,' Patricia mused. 'That, plus a "better the devil you know" attitude.' She cast another glance at the mirror frame. 'Actually, that's growing on me. It's rather arty. You should finish doing it.'

It seemed she had grown tired of exploring the past for now. Magnolia knew when to leave things well alone, so she continued playing around with the cogs and gears whilst Patricia fluttered companionably in the background. Twenty minutes later however, she was finished, and in the mood to see if she could find any other interesting items for the shop.

'Can I go and have a look in the outbuilding?'

'Why are you asking me? It doesn't belong to me anymore.'

'Well... I sort of feel as though it still does.'

Patricia shrugged. 'It's fine by me; are you wanting to see if there's anything interesting in there worth having, or are you wanting to clear it out?'

'Both, really.'

'I'll come with you.'

Although she'd had a brief nose around a few weeks ago, Magnolia hadn't yet explored the outbuilding properly. She'd been putting it off, actually, seeing it as a chore until now, rather than a chance to discover something intriguing. The interior wasn't as gloomy as she remembered it to be; perhaps last time had been a dull weather day, and it did have windows along two sides. However, it was extremely dusty. Magnolia sneezed, and then looked at Patricia.

'Doesn't it make you sneeze, coming in here?'

Patricia gave her a derisive look. 'Seriously?'

'Sorry… I forgot.'

Magnolia looked around the space appraisingly. 'We should do a stock check and when he comes back to the shop with the diving helmet for me, ask Nathan which items he wants, and which items we can chuck or re-home.'

'He closed the business knowing this place was still chock-a-block with stuff, so why should we bother seeing if he wants any of it now?'

'You've changed your tune.'

'I'm just being pragmatic.'

Magnolia took a few steps forward, and peered under a couple of protective sheets to see the treasures below. 'It's not as disorderly in here as I thought it would be, actually.'

'That's because we had respect for our antiques.'

Making her way over to the far wall, Magnolia noticed a toffee-coloured vintage leather suitcase. Its corners were elegantly curved, and it had wrap-around straps with decorative brass buckles. 'Oh, I love this!' she exclaimed, giving it a rudimentary dusting with her hand to see its pigment and condition more clearly. 'It's like a piece of luggage you'd see on the Orient Express years ago.'

'I can categorically confirm that it *has* been on the Orient Express… many years ago.'

'Don't start all that with me. Next, you'll be telling me that it belonged to Agatha Christie.'

'Don't be ridiculous. Agatha Christie never went on the Orient Express. She just wrote about it.'

'Of course she went on the Orient Express! That's the whole reason *Murder on the Orient Express* exists. The experience inspired her.'

Patricia suddenly looked a little unsure of herself.

'Anyway… whatever; I can't use it as a chocolate display feature, however beautiful it is, because it'll make my chocolates smell of leather.'

'Suit yourself.' Patricia wandered off to the other side of the building like a truculent toddler.

'Do you think there's anything inside it?' Magnolia called over to her from her crouched position near the floor.

Patricia floated back over. 'Don't know. Why don't you take a look?'

Magnolia unfastened the straps and flipped the clasp. She then raised the lid.

'*Raaaaaa*!' Patricia suddenly screeched in her ear.

Having been crouched on just her toes, Magnolia promptly toppled to one side in fright.

'What the hell!'

Patricia swooped forward. 'Don't crush the puzzle jug! It's eighteenth century!'

'Oh, I'll just crush my bones instead, shall I?' Magnolia looked up to see a jug with an ugly floral design — in her opinion — suspended in the air, courtesy of Patricia, a pattern of elaborate holes at its neck.

'Phew, saved it,' Patricia said, allowing it to return to the floor.

'That jug has actual holes all around its neck,' Magnolia stated, as she brushed dust and cobwebs from her dress.

'Yes — it's a puzzle jug, like I said,' Patricia responded exasperatedly. 'They're an example of our ancestors' cheeky sense of humour. They'd be brought out towards the end of dinner parties, when everyone was three sheets to the wind. The idea was to drink from the jug without spilling a drop; clearly a ludicrous undertaking. I pity the poor person who had to wash the tablecloth afterwards — especially if there was red wine in the jug.'

'Well pity me instead. I hope this dress cleans up properly.' Magnolia looked down at herself. Her dress, a favourite, was a smoky-blue light wool shift with *plumetis* tulle and lace panels sewn in. Not a dress to be exploring mouldering outbuildings in, she thought wryly.

'At least you haven't been stuck in the same bloody outfit for a couple of years,' Patricia responded sulkily.

"Yeah, you call top trumps again,' Magnolia conceded. 'Come on... let's go. I've had enough excitement for one day.'

Chapter Twenty-One

The next day, and they were in the kitchen; chocolate production had inevitably come back on the agenda.

'What are you making?' Patricia asked, taking in the cherries, kirsch and cream laid out on the worktop alongside the usual chocolate pellets.

'Black Forest gateau truffles.'

'Why on earth would you want to do that? What's the point?'

'Huh?'

'If someone wanted Black Forest gateau, then why wouldn't they just eat the gateau itself, rather than going for your truffles?'

'It's about the joy of the unexpected.'

'How can a chocolate taste like cake, anyway?'

'Well, that's the challenge, isn't it? It doesn't literally, absolutely taste like cake. But if you get the texture of the *ganache* just right, it can be quite a revelation.'

Patricia raised her eyebrows sarcastically. 'Right, I'll leave you to it, then.'

Magnolia's phoned buzzed. She wiped her hands on a cloth and checked it. Inquisitive as ever, Patricia hovered around in case the incoming notification heralded something worth knowing. 'Nathan's on his way over…in twenty minutes,' Magnolia declared, eyes wide. Something definitely worth knowing, Patricia determined joyfully.

The next twenty minutes were quite entertaining for Patricia, as Magnolia flitted around nervously, brushing her hair and smoothing it down, dabbing balm on her lips and lamenting about the loss of some sort of magic under-eye gel that she eventually located in "the wrong pocket" of her handbag, before hurriedly applying it. All this activity was wrapped up in pretence of nonchalance at Nathan's impending visit, and an attempt to convince Patricia that it was just a coincidence that these "usual daily habits" she was carrying out fell within the window of time before he arrived.

'It's a Siebe Gorman brass twelve-bolt top light diving helmet,' Nathan announced, lifting the treasure from its storage box with a flourish. 'It has a bit of a dent at the back, but you won't be able to see that if you display it in a certain way.'

'It's extraordinary! I love it! I'm going to put it up there.' Magnolia pointed to the top back corner of the shop, just behind the main serving counter, where it would also be viewable from the hot chocolate counter. 'I'll have a dedicated shelf made for it.'

'You're taking an antique that's spent most of its working life at the bottom of the sea and putting it at the top of the world instead?' Magnolia looked at him with wide, questioning eyes. Nathan laughed delightedly. 'I'm joking — it's the perfect place for it.'

Magnolia nudged his arm playfully and laughed in relief before looking thoughtful. 'I definitely got the best deal — a measly hot chocolate in exchange for a vintage brass diving helmet. Seems to me it's only right that I give you free chocolate forever.

'Actually... I've just made a *sachertorte*. I don't usually make cakes, but sometimes I do when the mood takes me. Would you like a slice? It's an Austrian chocolate cake; quite rich, but it has apricot jam in it to offset the richness a bit.'

'It sounds great, but I've no room for it right now,' he said, patting his stomach and looking a little regretful. 'I'd be cheeky, and ask for some to take away for later, but I can't really carry it. My mate owns a micro-brewery-slash-pub just down the road and I'm helping him out for a bit. I'm on my way there now to drop off those two boxes of glasses.' He inclined his head towards two thick cardboard boxes he'd brought in at the same time as the diving helmet box.

Magnolia shrugged nonchalantly. 'Well, it'll still be here later this afternoon if you want to call back for some. And I won't be up to my elbows in chocolate, so you won't be disturbing me. I need to do some boring cleaning instead — you're welcome to disturb that!'

He laughed. 'I might just do that.'

It was only after Nathan had left that Magnolia realised Patricia had been unusually absent throughout his visit. She couldn't decide whether that was a good thing or not.

Then she realised she'd forgotten to bring her laptop to the shop that day. It sat on the kitchen table at home; where she'd left it at around midnight, after a couple of hours editing photos of truffles and pralines for her website and social media posts. Having thought she didn't need it, she changed her mind at lunchtime. She didn't fancy taking on the challenge of the Black Forest gateau truffles anymore, nor the cleaning that she'd mentioned to Nathan, and could do with updating her supplier spreadsheet instead.

She decided to walk through the park on her way home. Patricia had resurfaced and started asking her uncomfortable questions about her opinion of Nathan; she didn't want to answer them and could do with clearing her head amongst the trees.

She paused by a patch of fiery Japanese maples. It was almost Halloween, and tell-tale signs of the celebration were dotted around the place; parents with pumpkins from the greengrocer's under their arms, or carrying bulging bags from the toy shop, with gauzy black netting spilling out over the top with the occasional flash of green or red fabric which also jostled out, destined to become fantastical Halloween costumes.

There was a definite nip in the air despite the low sun's brightness, and Magnolia pulled on her cashmere-soft fingerless gloves. A pair of nursery-age twins careened joyfully through the fallen leaves, kicking them up at each other, scuff-toed shoes evidence that this was a common pursuit. Green still fought with gold and amber on those trees that were still dressed, and the pond shimmered captivatingly with the riot of colour from their reflections.

It wasn't an unimpeded view of the pond for Magnolia, though; a man stood before it, gazing out, his figure a lean and sturdy capital "A", feet planted in military-style boots and his three-quarter-length herringbone tweed overcoat unbuttoned to the elements. She approached him, noticing as she did so the olive-green shade of the tweed coat; she knew before he turned around that the colour would bring out those gold flecks in his eyes. Was it him, or was she just projecting a fantasy of him?

He looked horrified to see her; Magnolia wondered why, and then noticed the half-eaten sandwich in his hand. 'Sorry' he said sheepishly. 'I'm sure your chocolate cake is amazing, but I needed something savoury and substantial. Are you offended?'

Magnolia laughed. 'Of course not! Do you think I eat nothing but sweet stuff? Caramel soup for lunch and chocolate lasagne for dinner?'

'Sweet pasta is definitely a thing. I had it in Italy; *mezze maniche* — which are pasta tubes, stuffed with sweet ricotta and topped with chocolate sauce. They're fried, which gives them a nice crispy texture.'

'Gee, thanks. I thought I was being cleverly witty. Now I feel stupid.'

'Don't feel stupid. Please don't think I'm a tiresome know-it-all either. I just like talking to you. But I end up saying the wrong things.'

'Well, *I* don't think they're the wrong things.'

They looked at each other and smiled. A leaf fell from a tree, caressing Magnolia's cheek on its way to the ground, and she wished it was Nathan's fingertips instead.

'I used to come here a lot when we had the shop,' Nathan mused. 'First time I've been back for months, though. I'm surprised it doesn't get busier. From a selfish point of view, I'm glad it's quiet, but I'm surprised. It's such a sweet burst of life and colour in contrast with all the sombre brick and stone of the High Street.'

'I think a lot of people assume it's a private garden. It doesn't exactly announce itself at the entrance. And it's set back into some sort of nook, so that's maybe why.'

An adorable French pug padded past them, proudly carrying a stick in his mouth that was easily a metre-long, and they shared a moment of delighted mirth.

'Actually, I used to come here to escape from my mum,' Nathan admitted ruefully.

Ah, the perpetual cycle of Patricia pushing people to the park, Magnolia thought wryly.

'It was originally my parents' antiques business,' Nathan continued. 'I only became involved when my dad died. Now Mum's passed away as well, and as much as this slice of nature kept me calm through some fraught times — we used to argue a lot, you see — I now wonder whether I should have stuck around more often and tried harder to sort things out with her.'

Magnolia was at a total loss what to say. How on earth could she tell Nathan that she knew more than he realised? That she'd heard his mum's side of the story direct from the ghost's mouth?

The self-important drake from the summer — when she'd made that life-changing phone call — waddled past; she liked to think it was the same one, anyway.

'Were you able to say a proper goodbye to your mum?' she asked Nathan carefully. He gave her a strange look, as though something was only just occurring to him.

'I thought so. But then… just recently… there was always some regret afterwards, but recently I've been having this odd feeling that there's some unfinished business between us after all.'

Magnolia had progressed from thinking she knew more than she should, to thinking she didn't know enough. She was confused. It didn't seem as though Nathan's regret was as torturous as to come from believing himself responsible for Patricia's death, which was good, but obviously it didn't tally with what Patricia had told her.

It was none of her business. Except Patricia had now made it her business. She hadn't just confided in her, she'd actively implored her to bring Nathan to the shop so she could make things right with him. But he'd been in the shop twice now, and Patricia had been strangely silent. And to top it all, the grumpy ghost's son had turned out to be far too distractingly attractive.

Magnolia had just realised she should be saying something comforting in response, when Nathan changed the subject anyway. 'Has chocolate making always been a big part of your life?' he asked.

They now stood on the section of path that curved around the pond and narrowed as it did so; two mothers with pushchairs approached, talking rapidly and oblivious to their surroundings, forcing Magnolia and Nathan to move breathtakingly closer. Magnolia caught the scent of him on the air; warm wood smoke with a twist of lemon. His enquiring eyes were too close, disarming her.

'Um, not in the beginning, despite my best efforts,' she said, drawing back shyly. 'I remember being about seven or eight, helping my mum carry the grocery shopping home during the school holidays with my brother, Mark. She didn't drive, so we always walked to the supermarket. At the small newsagent just near our house we'd usually stop for a treat as a reward for our efforts. I always wanted a bar of chocolate, but most of the time Mum wouldn't let me — we were only allowed to have a bag of sweets.

'I know, I should have been grateful — some poor children don't have any treats at all — and I was; but boiled, jelly, foamy lumps of sugar just didn't do it for me. I wanted sugar, yes — but I wanted that heavenly, velvety texture and hit of cocoa.' Magnolia sighed in reminiscence.

'Why did your mum want you to have sweets instead of chocolate?'

'Sweets last longer, especially the boiled ones, whereas chocolate is gone in the blink of an eye. Mum would always have a bar of dark chocolate filled with mint fondant. I thought it was so decadent. It had a foil inner wrapper that twinkled alluringly. She proved her point by eating it in just a few seconds. Our sweets lasted right up until bedtime. I'm sure her real motive was to keep us quiet with sweet-popping hamster cheeks all the way through her TV soap-watching fest.'

Nathan gave an unencumbered laugh. 'That's ridiculous!'

'Well... it's true though, isn't it? Sweets literally take longer to suck or chew than chocolate. Anyway, I guess wanting what I couldn't have set me on the path to cocoa obsession.'

There was a gust of wind; fallen leaves skittered across the ground like mice and Nathan's abundant hair blew out and away from his face. Magnolia imagined it would do the same if he was an Arthurian knight, in the sudden rush of his horse charging forward. *Bloody hell, pull yourself together.*

'Want half my sandwich?' Nathan offered. 'It'll probably go to the ducks, otherwise.'

Magnolia shook her head. 'No, thanks. I need to dash home to collect my laptop. But if you're sticking around here for the next few minutes, I could bring you that wedge of cake when I come back?'

'Sounds good. If you're walking back this way, though, I could come back to the shop with you?'

She was both relieved and disappointed that he didn't suggest walking her home. She couldn't decide whether it would be a bit too full-on if he did; yet she wanted to ask him about the vibe of the French and Italian cafés that he'd surely experienced in abundance during his time travelling over there, and enjoy the sense of him walking alongside her, without the exhausting eye contact.

'OK, great' she said, smiling. 'I'll see you in a bit, then.'

When Magnolia returned to the park, Nathan looked dead. He was sitting on a bench, his head thrown right back, as though he'd been shot. She rushed over, rather alarmed, to realise he was just watching the clouds.

'Look at that cloud!' he exclaimed, pointing at the twisting cumulus above them. 'Quite often you can see the shape of a griffin, or maybe a dragon, but that one's really unusual — it looks like a teapot in mid-pour.'

'It does!' Magnolia laughed. A small child on a bike had stopped in front of them, impatiently waiting for his mother to catch up. By the time she drew level, he was looking up at the clouds too.

'Look, Mummy, it's a teapot!' he enthused.

'Oh, yes! Aren't you clever,' his mother praised him. She secured a bag of apples that was threatening to tumble from the cage basket in front of his handlebars. As mother and son then moved on, Magnolia laughed again.

'Well, you've definitely influenced the younger generation there.'

'Crikey, it's a good thing he didn't pedal past five minutes earlier — I was singing a death metal song to myself.'

'It's a good thing I didn't come back at that point too — I'd have left you to it for sure.'

'In that case, I'll wait until you've given me that slice of chocolate cake before I next break into song.' She nudged his arm playfully as he rose from the bench, and they moved off together.

'What was the best thing about Paris?' she asked, as they walked back to the shop.

'For me, it wasn't anything as obvious as the Eiffel Tower or the Pont des Arts or the Louvre; stunning but stifling — too many people desperately trying to suck up the magic. For me, it was a neo-gothic bookshop at the end of an obscure, higgledy-piggledy street. I spent most of the winter in Paris sat by a hulking cast iron radiator in one of the reading rooms — they have several of them in the alcoves off the main hall —

reading *Dracula* in French until I had a reasonable grasp on the language.'

'Reading *Dracula* in a Parisian bookshop... that's so atmospheric. I really should learn another language. Are you fluent in French now then?'

'Not at all! I know just enough to muddle through a short, slow conversation. Actually living out there for a couple of months really does help, because you're fully immersed in it, but reading a much-loved book in the language you want to master is great if you want a change from the pressure and embarrassment of learning through verbal interaction.'

'A neo-gothic bookshop must be a lovely learning environment too,' Magnolia considered dreamily.

'It was exquisite: grand arches and columns framing glass-fronted bookcases... split levels and spiral staircases... ornately carved wood panelling... and the stained-glass windows! There was one in my favourite reading room. There was a week when it snowed in Paris every day, and every day I was there — hugging the radiator and reading beneath the window. The snow gradually piled up on the frame, and then against the glass, through the course of the day, ever so hypnotically.

'Have you seen any of those nature documentaries on TV featuring bioluminescent sea creatures? The way they meander through the ocean depths in a display of shifting colours was the effect of the drifting snow on the stained glass, if you watched closely enough.'

'Oh, I know just what you mean! Wow, I could listen to you talking about your travels for hours.'

They reached the main road that sliced through the High Street and stopped. An approaching car caught the sun's rays just so, and they both put a hand up to their eyes simultaneously, as it temporarily dazzled them. As they crossed the road and continued walking on the other side, Magnolia thought how unnatural it seemed not to be holding hands with Nathan; such was the sense of familiarity she felt with him, despite them having only recently met.

He'd gone quiet, so she looked across at him; he now had a different kind of faraway look in his eyes.

'I didn't get the opportunity to travel much when I was a kid…despite my parents — well, my dad — jetting to all sorts of places,' he mused.

Magnolia didn't know what to say. She was interested to hear him elaborate, but it felt as though she was cheating in some bizarre game, with Patricia having touched on Nathan's childhood.

He continued anyway.

'Dad, much more than Mum, sometimes went abroad to hunt for antiques. He liked his drink — rather too much, actually — and on weekend evenings he'd frequently entice me with detailed descriptions of which countries he was going to visit next and the adventures to be had there. And he'd always say he was going to take me with him. I'd sit there in awe of him for what seemed like hours, so captivated and excited about what was to come. At first, I didn't notice the rapidly diminishing level of liquid in the bottle in front of him; that realisation came in later years.

'The next day I'd rush to him, eager to pick up where we'd left off the night before in our travel plans. But he never remembered. He'd drink himself into such a stupor that he'd never remember the promises he made to me or the hope he'd instilled in me. It happened time and again, I'd believe him time and again… and it crushed me time and again; because he never honoured a single promise. He always made me out to be the fool for listening to him whilst he was "enjoying a bit of a drink".'

'That would be devastating to experience as an adult — I can't even imagine how much more so as a child,' Magnolia sympathised.

'Yes, it was, but…' Nathan shook his head rapidly, as though attempting to physically dislodge the memory. 'Sorry, I didn't mean to burden you with unfortunate tales of my childhood. That was a long-winded way of getting around to what I actually wanted to say. Which is, that I didn't get the chance to explore other countries until I became an adult — and I still feel as though I'm making up for lost time.'

He then told her about his extended stay in Siena — the highlight of his European wanderings. He'd rented a room from a truffle hunter for a couple of months, earning a generous discount on his room by

213

helping him sell autumnal white truffle butter, oil and honey, from a little stall just by the Torre del Mangia.

He told her about the charming architecture; buildings mostly in shades of peach and rose, the light itself seeming to glow with these same colours. He told her about the streets that seemed to stretch up and squeeze in, until spilling out onto the Piazza del Campo — the magnificent bowl of rosy brick ground that all the skirting buildings leaned in to, proclaiming this as the heart of the city.

They arrived at the shop and Magnolia blinked, disorientated. Nathan was patiently waiting for her to unlock the door, but she'd been blissfully lost in the world he'd conjured.

'I love what you've done with the shop, as I said last time, but even the kitchen looks good,' Nathan said, as he followed Magnolia past the hot chocolate counter and beyond. 'We only ever used it for making coffee and tea and toasting sandwiches.'

'The Pizza Pizzazz guys who had the place just before me did most of the work to make it a proper kitchen,' Magnolia responded, pulling a cake tin towards her. She opened it to reveal a small yet elaborate chocolate cake, probably only one portion's worth, an impressive ruffled fan of chocolate crowning the glossy icing.

'Damn, I can't have a slice of that!' Nathan exclaimed.

Magnolia laughed. 'Oh, this is the wrong one. It's a cake for my niece, Sophie. She asked if I'd make her a "grown-up" chocolate cake. Hence the fancy ruffle on top. The cake itself is just a basic sponge — nowhere near as rich as the *sachertorte*.'

'Wow! How did you make the ruffle?'

Magnolia retrieved an identical cake tin from a shelf on the other side of the kitchen, peering inside to check it was the correct one. 'You just temper some chocolate — that means heating chocolate and then cooling it again quickly to specific temperatures — and then use a palette knife to spread a thin rectangle of the melted chocolate on your work surface. Then, when it's not quite dried, you ruffle it up with the knife. It's still quite malleable at that stage, so then you can untighten the ruffles and fan it out a bit as you put it on the cake.'

Nathan looked impressed, yet a little dazed. 'Oh, right.'

'How interested are you in knowing how it's done? Only slightly or massively?'

'Why? Is that a trick question?'

Magnolia shrugged. 'No. It's just I could actually show you now. It doesn't take long.'

He grinned. 'In that case — massively.'

'OK,' Magnolia's eyes brightened. 'We'll make a ruffle for the *sachertorte*. It's not at all a traditional thing to do, but who cares? It's only us who'll be eating it.'

Minutes later, enveloped by the rich scent of gently melted chocolate, Magnolia and Nathan were working together to carefully construct the frilled decoration; their fingertips touching and sparking off each other fleetingly yet ever so delightfully in the course of their craft.

In the "garden that wasn't a garden", Patricia punched the air and danced a little jig on the spot.

Chapter Twenty-Two

It was a fresh day, and Magnolia was once again in the kitchen, having an experience equally as intense as last time, when Nathan had been with her, yet in a completely different way.

She was in the process of cleaning; she'd been working on a particularly complicated project — separate milk, dark, white, ruby and mint chocolate tempering required all for one creation — and every surface was coated in a film of leftover dried chocolate. She'd been trying to do too much at once, and more bowls, spatulas and cloths than usual had been used.

Patricia had attempted to help clean up, somehow convincing herself that she'd learnt how to sustain the continuous pressure and dexterity needed to swoosh a cloth or a mop. It soon became apparent that she hadn't. One-off strikes and yanks were fine — anything requiring a burst of continuous energy — but anything more subtle was still outside her repertoire. Nevertheless, she accompanied Magnolia throughout.

'Nathan had a girlfriend who hated trees,' Patricia now mused, seemingly from nowhere. 'She said she felt as though they were suffocating her. Don't you think that's ridiculous? Trees take in all our carbon dioxide and other harmful elements and breathe out oxygen for us to breathe in. It's the very antithesis of suffocation.'

Magnolia paused to contemplate this, the washing liquid bottle in her outstretched hand. 'That's sad... to feel that way. They're so cleansing. I suppose she just meant she felt as though they were physically closing in on her. Dense forests can have a malevolent effect like that sometimes.'

'Don't be nice about her. She was a real madam. There was that time when...'

'Stop!' Magnolia theatrically clamped her hands over her ears. 'I don't want to know.'

Patricia raised her eyebrows. 'Why?'

'Now that I've actually met Nathan, I think it's inappropriate for you to tell me things about him that he wouldn't choose to tell me himself. The dynamic is weird enough as it is without you telling me all his secrets. He doesn't know that I know you.'

Patricia cackled. 'That's fair enough.' She zoomed into the front of the shop, and over to one of the old water pipes repurposed as shelf brackets; gurning childishly at her reflection before zooming onwards to partake in one of her habitual nosing sessions at passers-by from the front window.

'Patricia?' Magnolia called, as she retreated. 'Just one thing... how likely do you think it is that he isn't married? I know you said he wasn't married when you were alive, but—'

Patricia turned around and smiled affectionately at her. 'He's not married, dear. He came close a couple of times, but — anyway, he's not.'

'Unless he had a whirlwind romance during these last few months with a gorgeous Parisian or Milanese girl and married her. You wouldn't know about that,' Magnolia pointed out.

'True. And everyone knows how stunning the girls from Paris and Milan are,' Patricia teased.

Magnolia looked stricken, though she tried to hide it by scraping away at a particularly stubborn lump of dried chocolate on the underside of the worktop lip.

'You're absolutely enchanting, Magnolia,' Patricia declared firmly, appearing at her elbow like an unfurling wisp of steam. Magnolia still hadn't quite got used to her uncanny movements. 'You're like a woodland fairy; all those bouncy locks and bright green eyes... and that fine bone structure. For God's sake, all you need is a pair of wings and a toadstool.'

'I could do with a magic wand, I know that much,' Magnolia grumbled. 'Everything's mashing my head in. I just want to fast-forward a month to when this place is open.' There was a pause, before a belated smile tugged at her mouth. She looked up at Patricia. 'Thanks for the compliment, though.'

Five minutes later, and she'd had a change of heart about discussing Nathan with Patricia. 'Tell me about Nathan when he was a lot younger?' she asked,

'Nothing too recent that'd be awkward for me to know, though.'

This request evidently pleased Patricia greatly. 'Even as a teenager — when he would have been forgiven for being hormonally moody and self-obsessed — he was overwhelmingly kind and considerate.

'We went on a family skiing holiday to the French Alps when he was seventeen — our last family holiday, as it transpired. Nathan had had a few lessons in the UK on a dry ski-slope during his last school year, so he was fairly proficient when we arrived in France. He also had youth on his side, of course.

'Eric was fairly unfit aerobically, but he had raw strength and a history of skiing as a child in his favour — he'd regularly skied over a couple of years in Switzerland whilst his father worked on a high-profile construction project over there. Switzerland had been their family home for the duration.

'And then there was me; ridiculously optimistic and lost in disillusionment. I was so high on the fact that Eric had pulled away from the booze long enough to consider, agree to, and then actually book the holiday, so wrapped up in thoughts of snow-dusted alpine forests, mountains made less foreboding by a whipped cream-like tumble of wondrous white softness, fragrant mulled wine and rich, oozing fondue in cosy log cabins, that it didn't even occur to me that I needed to actually learn to ski.

'When Eric realised how inept I was on the slopes, he didn't hang around. I do take some responsibility for not highlighting my shortcomings earlier, but in my defence, I didn't realise that the difference in our ability would affect our enjoyment in skiing together. I thought we could still somehow glide alongside each other, albeit at a different technical level, relishing the crisp air and the majestic, unsullied landscape together.

'It was wholly surprising to both me and Nathan just how incandescent with rage Eric became when it dawned on him that I wouldn't be able to ski the black runs.. He promptly departed to spend the next six days throwing himself down a few black runs — in Nathan's words, with minimal finesse yet maximum aggressive fearlessness — before ensconcing himself in a *bar* for four or five hours to consume copious quantities of wine and *Génépi*.

'Conversely, Nathan couldn't have been more patient and reassuring. We spent a while on the nursery slopes together, where he taught me the basics, including how to snowplough and use a button lift, and then we progressed to blue runs. He never once made me feel as though I was spoiling his holiday. He instinctively knew when to be serious and when to be funny; the moments to be calm and the moments to be exuberant.

'The more I learnt, the more I was able to relax and have fun swishing tentatively down the valley with Nathan. By the end of the week, we were following delightful, looping tracks through the trees, and I was able to look around me and really enjoy the scenery instead of my gaze being locked on my skis, with my teeth gritted. After a few hours of that, we sat on deckchairs with a beer each, on the balcony of a bar, three spectacular valleys unfurling below us, the sun hot on our faces, yet snow a metre-deep at our feet.

'In the evenings we'd either cook a one-pot wonder or go out to a restaurant, before returning to the apartment to play cards. Eric was often an empty husk, but sometimes he'd engage with us quite pleasantly; which never lasted long, but we made the most of it whilst it did.

'It was a hotchpotch of a holiday. On the one hand, Eric drifted further away from us, but on the other hand, the relationship between Nathan and I gained a new facet.'

Patricia seemed to snap out of her reverie and her outline flickered a little with the change in energy. 'Anyway… this has turned into a bit of a whinge about Eric, and that wasn't my intention. I was merely trying to highlight Nathan's lovely character.'

'I understand. Sometimes a particular situation brings out the worst in one person whilst simultaneously bringing out the best in another person. Or, someone's positive attributes are brought to the fore in reaction to someone else's negative attributes.'

'Yes, that's absolutely right.' Patricia seemed stunned that Magnolia had understood her point, wrapped up as it had been in reminiscence of her one and only skiing adventure. She beamed. 'So...what do *you* think of Nathan?' she asked, with faux lightness. Magnolia had sensed this coming, but still wasn't any better prepared with an answer. She was in the process of loading the dishwasher with chocolate-encrusted paraphernalia, but she stopped to give the question her full attention.

'He's...unlike anyone I've ever met before. He seems keen to share the way he sees the world with people, to share what's important to him... to discover what's important to you and enthusiastically explore the similarities and differences, without making out he's any kind of expert or self-aggrandising.'

That doesn't go anywhere near far enough in describing him, Magnolia chided herself.

Patricia looked at her, lost for words.

'Have I said something wrong?' Magnolia asked anxiously.

'No — what you said is so right that it's taken me by surprise. I've forgotten what I was going to ask you next, now.'

Magnolia continued rattling around with kitchen implements; Patricia continued floating, disconcertingly now, with a pondering look on her face. Neither of them spoke for a minute or so.

'Who would be your ideal man?'

And there it was. Magnolia should have known that they were heading down this track. Patricia had a habit

223

of assuming that a momentary silence in a conversation wiped out Magnolia's memory of what they'd been talking about before the pause; that no connection could be made simply by following the trail of previous questions as to what her underlying purpose was. Squirming a little at the question, Magnolia procrastinated by turning away from Patricia and scooping rogue freeze-dried strawberries into the palm of her hand, and then depositing them in the bin. It was too difficult to answer.

'Remember when we were sitting in the garden — before the heather and lavender pots, when my shelving was being fitted? And you didn't want to talk about what you missed most about being alive?'

'Yes?'

'Well... I don't want to talk about my ideal man.'

'OK. I respect your wishes.'

'Good. Thank you.' In a show of snapping closed the subject, Magnolia snapped closed the fastener on the three five-kilo sacks of chocolate pellets she'd been using. Patricia silently watched her put them away in the pantry, with a look of pensiveness and more than a little knowing on her face.

Chapter Twenty-Three

In the early hours of the morning, trying in vain to sleep, Magnolia was in the grip of sudden anxiety. What had made her think she could be a successful *chocolatier?* What had possessed her to think she could make a living out of it? What if she developed regular, random coughing fits that threatened the hygiene of her kitchen and deterred potential customers if they heard her spluttering? What if the ambient temperature of the shop got too hot in the summer or too cold in the winter and affected the quality of her produce on the shelves?

She could feel her heartbeat thumping too quickly as her mind whirred faster and faster through possible catastrophes like a crazed Victorian zoetrope. As she tried to find a comfortable sleeping position, her body suddenly seemed too angular and alien and her feet incomprehensibly started twitching. She refused to look at the time to check just how long she'd been lying there — didn't the experts say that constantly checking the time psychologically compounded the problem?

Then there was Patricia. How could she run the shop with Patricia wandering in the background? Once she opened to the public, something weird that she couldn't explain away to people was bound to happen eventually. On the other hand, she'd miss her support and friendship. She didn't want her to go.

She refused to think about Nathan; that really would mess everything up.

Then, as the encroaching dawn stretched its milky fingers through her bedroom window, Magnolia began to find solace in the memory of how she'd regained her confidence in the world of chocolate... her heartbeat slowed down and she finally drifted into blessed sleep with the memory cradling her in its curling, soothing wispiness.

The wedding, six years previously...

Claire and Mark's bohemian wedding was a fresh and breezy, elegant delight. Held in Claire's parents' generous garden, it was a joyful celebration of love, adorned with tumbling garlands of fragrant eucalyptus, sage and boxwood at every turn — from the ceremonial backdrop to the dining table decorations.

The cake was a three-tier stack of naked Victoria sponges, bulging with fresh cream and dotted here and there with charming little fresh succulents. There were macramé-decorated jam jars and tiny bud vases of wildflowers attached to guests' chairs and hanging from anything they could conceivably be hung from.

The day unfurled in a haze of wonder after wonder; Claire looked ethereal in a white dress with a relaxed, free-flowing shape yet comprised of exquisite lace with elaborate fringe detail. She held a loose bouquet of ferns, eucalyptus and sage, with the occasional anemone and peony, and had a similar style headdress crowning her bouncy hair.

After the wedding breakfast but before the dancing, most guests left the marquee to enjoy the gardens and mingle with each other. Bales of straw draped with colourful blankets had been loosely positioned to encourage the sitting of cosy groups, and a VW campervan converted to a gin bar and an Austin Mini converted to an ice-cream van were positioned at a jaunty 45-degree angle to each other by a copse of trees festooned with tiny fairy lights.

Magnolia and Mark had just escaped from their parents' smug endorsement of their holiday home in Alcudia; it was a monologue they'd heard countless times previously, right down to the painful detail of which local supermarket sold the cheapest chorizo, so they'd left Claire and her parents to be ensnared on their own.

'Good day so far?' Magnolia asked, blocking the sun with her hand to look at her brother as she sank down onto a bale.

'Amazing. Nowhere near as stressful as I thought it'd be. And Claire obviously looks stunning. I'm just a bit confused by all the floral and fruity stuff.'

Magnolia laughed. 'Given that I'm named after a flower, do you really think you should be saying that to me? Anyway, I think it's perfect. All the greenery really freshens up the effect of the flowers.'

'Yeah, but all the gins and ice-creams have either got fruit or flowers in them.'

'That's true. But it fits with the whole feel of the day. You must have discussed it with Claire countless times when you were planning the wedding.'

'I guess so.'

'I think it's wonderful.' Magnolia leaned back dreamily on her straw bale, quickly remembered it had no back support, and righted herself.

'At least the music was my choice.'

Magnolia chuckled. 'Only because Adio agreed with you!' Adio was Claire's father. His roots were Jamaican, and he wholeheartedly approved of Mark's love of reggae music. Mark harrumphed and wiped his hand across his forehead.

'Find me an ice-cream that doesn't have fruit in it, Nolls?' he implored her.

She retrieved her kicked-off shoes, smoothed the creases from her *eau de nil* floaty dress, and stood.

'You know I'm only doing as you ask because it's your big day, don't you?' she said, playfully, not waiting for a response before padding across the grass with as much elegance as her bound-to-sink stiletto heels allowed.

She scanned the menu board, realising that an ice-cream without fruit would indeed be a big ask. Damn, they all sounded delicious, though: apricot and lemon thyme, blueberry crumble, strawberry and mint, passion fruit cheesecake. Banoffee pie was the best bet — looking at it, the generous swirls of toffee sauce and crumbly biscuit would probably distract Mark from the banana. She asked for one, then cast a glance at the gin bar for herself. She couldn't see the menu, but Mark had a point there too, judging by the various combinations of berries and foliage bobbing about in the ice-packed goblets of the guests milling around the area.

She returned with Mark's ice-cream, and a delicious lavender and lime gin for herself, to find a woman in a striped red and black dress, complete with biker boots and long, black hair, sitting on her straw bale. She recognised her from several times earlier in the day because she was so fabulously incongruous.

'Sorry I pinched your bale!' The woman spoke in a bright voice, shuffling along to make room for Magnolia. 'I'm Colette. I'm a friend of Claire's from way back when her family lived in Manchester.'

'Hi, good to meet you,' Magnolia smiled. 'Is that your partner over there, looking for you?' She pointed at a very tall, thin man with very straight jaw-length hair in a crumpled linen suit, looking panicked by the ice-cream Mini. She remembered seeing them together earlier.

Colette waved her hand dismissively. 'Jake's fine. He's not looking for me... he's actually trying to escape from me.'

Mark found this hilarious, and gave a great guffaw. Magnolia laughed too. 'Sorry. I'm Magnolia, by the way,' she belatedly introduced herself.

'Ooo, I know you are,' Colette enthused. 'That's why I made a beeline for you. Your chocolates are absolutely amazing. Claire told me you don't do it for a living — which you should, by the way! — but I was hoping you might consider making my wedding favours? I'm getting married in a couple of months. I'd pay you, of course.'

'I'd love to!' Magnolia was delighted. 'What flavours and types of chocolate do you like?'

'Well, the ones you made for today were exquisite, but maybe something a little less floral?'

'Thank you!' Mark slapped his palm to his knee triumphantly.

For Claire and Mark's wedding favours Magnolia had made elderflower and prosecco truffles, enrobed in white chocolate and rolled in edible flower petals — a mix of blue cornflower, orange marigold and pink rose.

'It's just that we're getting married in a haunted castle,' Colette continued, 'and as you can see, I'm more of a goth than a woodland elf, so…'

'How about a slightly more intense flavour and look?' Magnolia suggested. 'I could do the same truffles as today, enrobed in dark chocolate and rolled in dried raspberry dust instead. Or I could do a black cherry and prosecco truffle. I could shape them like little coffins or skulls, if you like.'

Colette, her husband Jared and their wedding guests had been thrilled with the black cherry and rum truffles shaped like mini coffins that Colette finally decided upon; as a result, two guests approached Magnolia with special requests.

The first was another wedding commission — a collaboration with the pâtissier creating the wedding cake. The bride wanted one-hundred heart-shaped passionfruit and prosecco truffles artfully "scattered" over the cake. Magnolia painstakingly attached slithers of edible gold leaf to each white chocolate-coated heart, and she and the pâtissier shared the task of attaching them to the cake.

The second commission was for a baby shower. The mother-to-be was expecting a boy; she was ecstatic at the giant marshmallow lollipops that Magnolia created for her party guests — a rosette of pale blue marshmallows drowned in white chocolate.

Magnolia's re-immersion in the world of chocolate making began there and then.

Chapter Twenty-Four

After snatching a meagre three hours' post-dawn sleep, Magnolia was bleary-eyed, sluggish, and hankering for a change to her usual routine. It was Sunday, and deciding she'd have a rest from preparing to open the chocolate shop, she phoned Claire with an appeal to be rescued.

They decided to go for a walk in the nearby woodland; some of the trees still held their amber crowns, and a morning frost combined with a burst of low winter sun created a dazzling effect like fire and ice in combat.

'Oh, did that Nathan-guy come back yet with the vintage diving helmet?' Claire asked, as Sophie joyfully skipped ahead in pursuit of a squirrel; it darted into a patch of ice-silvered bracken, whilst Sophie looked on, perplexed as to why it hadn't wanted to stick around.

'Yep,' Magnolia responded, watching a few fallen leaves dance around her boots with each step, as the light breeze ruffled the top layer of the forest floor where sun rather than ice had penetrated.

'And?'

'I showed him how to make a chocolate ruffle.'

'What?'

'A chocolate ruffle. I showed him how to temper chocolate, and we had a quick sort of... crafting class.'

'Are you *serious*?' Claire stopped walking and stared at Magnolia incredulously.

'Yes. Why are you so shocked? You'd think I'd just told you we had impulsive sex on the kitchen counter!' She'd checked Sophie was well out of earshot before retorting with this.

'Well, it is just as shocking as that! You've never shown anyone how you create magic in the kitchen. You've always kept it such a big secret!'

'You make my chocolate making sound so nefarious.'

Claire put her hand on Magnolia's arm and swung her around to face her. 'Nolly, it's just that you've always kept people at a distance from you in that regard. It's just... momentous that you've shared that part of you with someone. You must really have a connection with him.' Claire smiled excitedly, eyes shining.

Magnolia rubbed her face with both hands and shook her head, not quite vehemently enough to indicate denial.

'So then what happened, after you made chocolate together?'

'Mark and Sophie interrupted us, just at the end, when they came to collect the "grown-up" cake. They were both banging on the window as we were washing the pots.'

Claire's mouth fell open in dismay. 'So you didn't get the chance to kiss him or anything?'

'Our fingertips touched a few times more often than necessary during the swishing of the chocolate, but that's all. It was quite embarrassing, actually. I don't mean that bit. As you've just said, I've never shown anyone how I work with chocolate before, so Sophie was quite put out. She wanted a lesson there and then. And Mark thought it was highly entertaining. I'm surprised he didn't tell you all this himself.'

'I'm sure he would have done, but I wasn't home most of last night. I was at some mind-numbing cosmetics party. At least there was wine there; I think it was supposed to make us more likely to buy stuff, but it just made me want to draw a Joker smile on the rep's face. Anyway, then Mark was out first thing this morning, so we didn't really see each other. I wondered what Sophie was chuntering on about though when I was trying to make her eat breakfast earlier.'

Sophie skipped over to them, her cheeks two rosy, plump apples from the cold, one pigtail unravelling over her shoulder. 'Are you coming home with us, Auntie Nolly?' she enquired. 'I won't be angry with you for not showing me the chocolate making if you make glitter fish with me instead.'

'Glitter fish?' Magnolia looked at Claire for clarification.

Her sister-in-law groaned. 'One of Mark's great ideas; drawing fish on cardboard, dousing them with a truckload of glitter, cutting them out, then attaching string and dangling them from every surface imaginable. It makes you think you're under the sea, apparently.'

'Sounds like fun! Yeah, I'm up for a bit of that.'

'Yay!' Sophie punched the air victoriously and skipped ahead of them again.

'How far do you want to walk?' Magnolia asked. 'As far as the tree that looks like a gargoyle, or up onto the moor? Although I suppose Sophie wouldn't be able to manage that.'

'Never mind Sophie — I'd struggle to manage that myself today, after all that wine last night. And there's no way I'm carrying her, either. Let's turn back at the gargoyle tree.'

'OK.'

They walked for a few moments in companionable silence, just taking in the sounds of the forest. As well as the intermittent crow and clack of pheasants in the undergrowth — it seemed Sophie couldn't scare every single one of them — there was an eerie sound, like wailing lost souls, emitting from the spindly silver birches towering above, as they caught the wind. Curiously, Magnolia found this captivating rather than creepy. Patricia must have completely skewed her menace radar.

She decided to cautiously elaborate on her feelings for Nathan — maybe Claire could make some sense of it all.

'So, this Nathan guy — he's a bit intense.'

Claire laughed. 'You do realise you said that the last two guys were a bit shallow? I think you're just looking for any excuse to write him off. For someone so keen to take a chance in the chocolate world, you're remarkably closed off to the same concept in your love life.'

Claire paused, as Sophie ran towards her clutching a handful of fallen leaves; she gave them to her mother for safe keeping — they were destined for some arty project no doubt — before running off again.

'The reason every relationship you've had has gone the same way is because you keep choosing guys based purely on the likelihood of them not making a fuss about you going off and doing your own thing for great swathes of time,' Claire continued. 'Don't mistake acquiescence — or even worse, indifference — for compatibility though.'

'But it's healthy to have time out doing separate things in a relationship.'

'Of course, but not to the extent that the guy barely has any impact on your life, and vice versa. It shouldn't be the key attribute of your relationship. It's like you just want to put them in a neat little box and only bring them out when it's convenient. Sorry, that's a bit harsh… I just mean that you never get truly close to someone — because you don't allow them to contribute to and share in the things that are important to you.'

'They never seem to want to contribute to and share in the things that are important to me, anyway.'

'That's because you choose the indifferent guy rather than the compatible guy. Having some differences is normal, as long as you have a strong foundation of common beliefs and passions. If you have that, then the little differences don't have to be annoyances; they can be like… like the seasoning… the salt and pepper, or the sugar… they can make everything so much richer. Sometimes it's good to let him go off… I don't know, zorbing, or whatever alone, and sometimes it's good to go with him to do the zorbing together; to discover something fresh and fabulous that you might never have otherwise experienced. Then again, if zorbing is completely against your moral code, then you need to question the relationship.'

'Is zorbing that thing where you crawl into a giant hamster ball and roll down a hill in it?

'Yes, but that's not the point.'

'Next time it'd be more helpful if you chose a less obscure example.'

'OK — duly noted.'

'You are being really helpful, though. I knew you would be. You're so much wiser and more with it than me.'

Claire shrugged. 'No, I'm not. Sometimes it's easier to see the pertinent issues when you're looking at the situation from a distance. And it's only since being with Mark that I realise what generally makes a lasting relationship.'

There was a break in the trees, revealing the moorland stretching majestically upwards, and Magnolia's thoughts turned to how much Patricia would love to be here to see it — even in the stark winter when it wasn't dressed in purple and popping against a bright sky.

They reached the stile at their turning-back point, and Claire beckoned for Sophie — a few metres off to the right — to follow them. She suddenly turned to make eye contact with Magnolia. 'Don't mess this one up, Nolly,' she said, surprisingly sternly.

'Huh?'

'Don't pretend that you don't know. I can see that he's right for you.'

'How? You've never even met him!'

'I don't need to. I can see it in your eyes when you talk about him. You're being conservative with your words, but the only other time I've seen that peculiar sparkle in your eyes is when you talk about a new chocolate recipe.'

A bird took flight from a nearby tree as they approached, sending an ice flurry of silvery sparkles to the ground. Magnolia clutched Claire by the arm; Claire thought she was reacting to the sudden movement of the bird, until continuing to hold onto her arm, Magnolia hugged her close in a walking side-embrace, and she realised it was a show of affection.

'I don't want to mess this one up, Claire,' she said quietly yet fervently. 'I really don't.'

'I'll help you not to,' Claire replied, hugging her sister-in-law back. 'I'll keep on at you about it.'

They gave each other a final squeeze before letting go.

'Changing the subject, is it still OK for Sophie to help me give out free chocolates a week on Saturday?' Magnolia asked. To promote the shop the week before opening, she was planning to make a couple of batches of chocolates especially for offering to passers-by on the High Street.

'Yep, she can wear the coat I've just bought for her,' Claire replied. 'She'll look adorable. It's a rich red double-breasted coat that flares out at the waist like a dress, and, get this — it has appliqué Christmas trees all around the bottom. Give her a big, shiny platter of chocolates to hand out at the shop door and stick a Santa hat on her head and she'll draw the crowds for sure.'

'I'm so glad you've embraced the child-exploitation angle of my promotional campaign,' Magnolia said ironically. Claire laughed and rummaged around in her pocket for her lip balm.

'It might be best to give her a tray of chocolates that she doesn't like, now that I think about it. Maybe dark chocolates with something a bit perfume-y, like rose or bergamot?'

'Why?'

'She'll probably eat them all, otherwise.'

239

'Isn't it a bit mean, purposely asking her to hand out chocolates that she doesn't like? Part of the joy and reward of doing it was supposed to be that she gets to sample the goodies. She'll be so disappointed if they're "horrible chocolates". She'll probably look really glum and scare everyone away. Anyway, I need to give out chocolates that represent my core product line; and they need to be seasonal.'

This time, Claire laughed even more exuberantly, her suddenly expelled breath a dancing chain of clouds in the cold air. 'OK, I'm with you. You're right,' she conceded. 'You'd better keep an eye on her, though. Make sure she doesn't snaffle too many.'

Chapter Twenty-Five

The weather had noticeably moved on. It was snowing, and there was also a fresh wind. As Magnolia walked to the shop, the fallen snow whipped up by the wind began to trail animatedly across the pavements and roads like frenzied white grass snakes. The early morning sky bore a blush the colour of the Turkish delight she'd been dipping in chocolate the day before, and the trees were splendidly dressed in white.

As cars manoeuvred towards the High Street, she felt grateful that she didn't have to drive to work anymore and contend with the inevitable anxiety she'd have over safety in these conditions. There was a flap and a flump as a bird took flight from a berry-rich rowan tree, both the sound and the motion startling Magnolia in the otherwise peaceful surroundings.

At the start of the High Street, the small café renowned for its English breakfasts, bacon buns, strong coffee and even stronger tea, was already doing a roaring trade. It seemed the sudden plunge in temperatures had brought out the human instinct to fill up on sustaining, comforting, calorie-laden foods.

Approaching the shop, she considered that this weather would be good for hot chocolate sales. She'd have to make sure the pavement just outside was kept clear of snow and ice though, and the shop floor would constantly have to be mopped on days like this, too. Maybe she should sell milkshakes in the summer, when hot chocolate sales would be low? Just chocolate and vanilla, though? She didn't want to move too far away from chocolate in general.

As she entered the shop, the key struggling to click in the ice-cold lock, and discarded her hat, scarf and gloves in a heap of butter-yellow cashmere on the counter, Patricia appeared. Magnolia caught a sense of excitement on the air.

'Magnolia, you have to come outside and see this!' Patricia insisted, hopping from one foot to the other in excitement.

'It's snowing, I know. I've just walked here in it.'

'Yes, but this is something entirely different.'

'Well in that case, can't it wait until I warm up a bit?'

'No! It's still snow-related. And it might stop if we wait too long.'

Magnolia just wanted to sit and hug the radiator for a while, with a hot coffee close by, but she reluctantly followed Patricia through the kitchen.

'Do you remember what happens if I stand in the rain?' Patricia asked, as Magnolia unlocked the back door.

'Yes. It just runs straight through you… and you don't get wet.'

'Well... watch this!' Not needing to float through the closed door in her usual manner, seeing as Magnolia had opened it anyway, Patricia saved her paranormal antics for the snow. 'Watch this!' she repeated, now that she was in position.

Magnolia watched. She was awe-struck. By now, she'd experienced a plethora of surprising, funny, slightly creepy, confusing, and impressive phenomena courtesy of Patricia — but never anything as beautiful as this.

As Patricia stood amongst the past-their-best terracotta pots, each fluffy, silver-white snowflake that pirouetted towards her from the sky elegantly alighted on her. They didn't quickly melt away, as they would on a warm-blooded human, and they didn't fall straight through her, as raindrops had always done. They stayed there. As her form was semi-transparent, yet the snowflakes adhered to her, the effect was an arresting outline of a woman comprised of thousands of brilliant diamonds.

'Pretty cool, huh?' Patricia extended her arms to take in the effect for herself.

'I don't know what to say... it's so... special.'

'Are you crying?'

'God, yeah, I am. I'm a bit overwhelmed. You look like a strange, beautiful angel.'

Patricia twirled around a little, accentuating the effect. For quite a few minutes they stayed there, enjoying the display that Patricia created, before she finally declared, 'OK, that's enough. Let's go inside now. I'm bored.'

Back inside, the snowflakes gradually fell from Patricia to the floor, where they then faded away; though the visual splendour was never to fade from Magnolia's memory.

Chapter Twenty-Six

Fizzing with purpose, Magnolia snapped up her apron and gathered her apparatus. Today was "Operation Christmas". First up, she wanted to construct three-D gift boxes made entirely from slabs of chocolate melded together; about the size of a fist, they would contain a selection of surprise treats. But should she tie real ribbon bows around them, or use coloured melted chocolate to pipe on pretend bows? She'd have to try both and see which looked best.

After a couple of hours, realising she was becoming irritable and sloppy as her fingers started to feel increasingly like bananas, she decided to adopt the "a change is as good as a rest" approach. She left the partially-constructed chocolate boxes for a while, and began making *marron glacés* instead.

Patricia wandered over just as she'd laid out a four-foot-long procession of trays boasting neat rows of the chestnuts in their glossy caramel coats. She intended to also add a coat of chocolate once they'd cooled.

'Wow, it's like a dissecting laboratory in here,' Patricia declared disparagingly, eyeing the treats with distaste. Magnolia furrowed her brow questioningly, so she elaborated. 'It's like the day at school that the science teacher made us all dissect sparrow brains.'

'Oh, charming! Remind me not to let you serve any customers when the shop opens.'

'Don't be ridiculous, Magnolia.'

Magnolia was just about to make a sarcastic retort, when there was a knock on the shop door. She sensed it was Nathan just by the shape and body language of his shadow. 'It's Nathan. Stay here!' she hissed at Patricia; then seeing her hurt expression, added rather more beseechingly, 'Please?'

Patricia nodded.

She didn't know what she expected when she opened the door to him, but she certainly didn't expect what she got — cold detachment. 'How are you?' she asked, searching his eyes for some sort of explanation... or at least warmth.

He didn't answer the question directly, but his response proved to be all the answer needed: 'So... quite a few people are saying this place is haunted.' His wonderful gold-flecked eyes met hers as he spoke, meaning she was doubly taken aback.

'Oh... right' she responded vaguely.

'Not just haunted by any old ghost either... they say it's the ghost of my mother.' He spoke casually, and so Magnolia found it difficult to gauge his opinion or motivation in opening the conversation. Only the eye contact hinted at the possibility that whatever she said next was going to be significant to him.

She didn't say anything.

'I just wondered what you thought about that. You must have heard the rumours? The guys at the brewery say it's been the talk of the High Street for months.'

She shrugged in a display of nonchalance. 'Yes. It doesn't bother me.'

'What — it doesn't bother you because you don't believe there's a ghost?'

There was a prolonged pause.

'No. It doesn't bother me because the ghost, Patricia, is a really lovely lady.'

Nathan laughed with harsh incredulity. 'Are you making fun of me?'

'No, I'm not. I wouldn't joke about something like this. I know how it was at the end for you both. I wouldn't be so insensitive as to joke about your mum's ghost.'

His eyes narrowed. 'Who have you been talking to about me?'

'No one! I mean… just Patricia.' Magnolia's voice trailed away weakly as she realised how she sounded.

'I can't decide whether you're crazy or trying to manipulate me,' he retorted carelessly. 'I've definitely made a mistake about your character, either way, so I think it's best if we don't see each other again.'

'What possible reason would I have for manipulating you?'

Suddenly Nathan's gaze switched to a point just beyond Magnolia, and his mouth fell open. Magnolia turned to see Patricia hurrying towards them with a three-kilo drum of cocoa powder in her arms. Quickly realising that, to Nathan, it must seem as though the drum was dancing through the air, she merely watched and waited for the show to unfold.

Ripping the lid off the drum with great gusto, then piercing the foil seal beneath with a fist punch, Patricia up-ended the contents onto the hot chocolate bar. The empty drum was then thrown to the floor with a flourish. Dumbfounded, Nathan stared at the ensuing mountain of cocoa, its peak gradually diminishing under the force of Patricia's hands until a smooth expanse of the dark powder coated the whole surface area of the counter.

Coughing a little on the airborne dust, both Nathan and Magnolia watched as letters began to emerge from the powder, Magnolia having the added benefit of seeing Patricia's forefinger act as the rudimentary writing instrument. The letters became words, until they read:

I'm sorry, Nathan. It wasn't your fault.

Nathan glared at Magnolia. 'How did you do that?' he demanded, eyes flashing angrily.

'I didn't do anything!' she responded indignantly. 'How could I have?' Patricia wasn't finished, though. Next came:

Apples and pears and sweet honey bears.

Nathan paled and buckled, grabbing at the counter for support. 'No one else would know those words,' he said quietly. Stepping backwards, he slid slowly down the wall to the floor and sat with his knees pulled up to his chest. He put his hand to his forehead in incomprehension; it left a cocoa powder palm print, from when he'd grabbed onto the counter.

He looked up at Magnolia. 'Mum used to say those words to me when I was little, just before I went to sleep. She'd make up her own stories about fantasy lands filled with wonderful creatures and exciting terrains… and delicious foods. At the end, just as I was drifting off, she'd say those words as she left my room.'

Magnolia bit her lip. She looked sideways at Patricia and saw tears glistening on her cheeks. Nathan followed her gaze until his eyes were directed right at his mother without him realising it.

'Mum?' he finally said, his voice cracked with emotion. Suddenly Magnolia felt a subtle change in the energy flow around them. Nathan's eyes widened and seemed to focus anew.

'Surely not,' Magnolia whispered.

'My darling boy!' Patricia exclaimed, as incredibly, they reached out for each other.

'I see you!'

'You see me!'

Their voices overlapped joyfully.

Then they embraced each other, as though Patricia had attained solidity; a weird yellow-purple light pulsing around them.

'It wasn't your fault!' Patricia insisted, as they drew apart and looked at each other in amazement.

'Mum, I already knew!' Nathan responded, equally vehemently. 'Towards the end, you admitted that you'd trashed the shop. You apologised over and over for blaming me for your fall. You apologised for everything. They were dosing you up with morphine quite regularly, so maybe that's why you don't remember.'

Patricia stilled.

'You apologised for everything,' Nathan reiterated. 'But the important thing is, I was just as at fault as you, overall. What happened to us? We used to be so close. How did it all fall apart?'

'I really don't know, darling. I'm just so glad that we've had this chance to put it back together,' Patricia said, embracing him once again; obviously delighted by their renewed closeness.

'Why are you still here?' Magnolia suddenly wondered aloud.

'Oh, charming!' Patricia huffed.

'You know I don't mean it like that. I just mean… weren't you supposed to cross over once you'd made peace with Nathan?'

The three of them looked at each other, then, ridiculously, up at the ceiling — as if expecting to see a shaft of brilliant light or a spiral of tiny celestial stars emerging to facilitate Patricia's transcendence. When still nothing happened, Magnolia rubbed her eyes wearily and sighed.

'Well, it would be nice if a booming voice from above could let us know what the situation is,' she said, irritably.

'The situation?'

'Your estimated time of departure.'

'I didn't realise you were so desperate to get rid of me.'

'I'm not! I just don't like all this uncertainty and sense of waiting for something. Surely you feel the same?'

Patricia nodded slowly. 'Can I try to give you a hug? See if I can? It just worked with Nathan.'

Nathan looked a bit wide-eyed again, as if the enormity of the experience was only just fully sinking in. Magnolia stepped forward to meet Patricia's outstretched arms, and expecting a chilly wispiness to enfold her, was instead pleasantly drawn into a warm and extraordinarily comforting embrace. It felt so good to finally have this contact with her friend.

'He didn't mean what he said. It's a lot for him to take in,' Patricia whispered in her ear. 'Trust me, he really likes you.'

All this did was serve to remind Magnolia of how hurtful Nathan had been in the moments before Patricia started flinging cocoa powder around. She broke away from Patricia with a sad smile and shook her head slightly.

'I'll leave you two to have some privacy to say everything you want to say,' she announced. 'I'll lock the shop door now, but the back door through the kitchen can be locked from the inside. When you're ready to go, Nathan, just go out the back and Patricia can lock up behind you.' She looked at Patricia. 'Well... that's if you don't cross over tonight after all. If you do, I'm not too bothered about anything in here being properly secure. There's nothing worth taking anyway.'

Patricia followed Magnolia to the shop door. 'I won't be crossing over tonight,' she said confidently. 'So, I'll see you tomorrow.'

'How can you be so sure?'

'I just know. It won't be much longer before I do... but I just know it's not tonight.'

'Um, OK. See you tomorrow, then.' Magnolia stepped outside and locked the door behind her whilst purposely avoiding eye contact with Nathan.

The High Street sparkled in the darkness. Christmas decorations would appear in the next week or so, but right now, a bewitching frost had settled on the surfaces — pavement, benches, bike racks and bins glistening with magical clarity instead of looming menacingly from the shadows. Further along, the occasional warm glow from a restaurant or late-closing shop spilled forth.

Welcoming the slight bite of cold on her face, Magnolia decided to walk to the small Italian deli-bistro three hundred metres along. She'd treat herself to a fresh squash and sage ravioli to take away and maybe have a glass of prosecco whilst she waited; lovely things that she hoped would act as a soothing balm against Nathan's harsh words when he'd arrived at the shop.

Chapter Twenty-Seven

Magnolia felt head-nodding tired. It was a cloud racing, skirt flapping, rubbish chasing kind of weather day, so she opened the shop door and simply stood on the doorstep awhile to get a blast of reinvigorating air. She needed to do this more often — seek out a breath of fresh air to deal with her weariness — rather than relying on endless mugs of coffee and hot chocolate.

Today, the morning after Patricia's big reveal to Nathan, she'd planned to spend populating the shop shelves with produce and taking photographs of the finished result. Thankfully, it was an activity that wouldn't require a great deal of concentration, yet would hopefully be very visually appealing by the end; she really couldn't cope with anything that required complex thought today — she was too emotionally raw.

She'd brought two lamps from home as well as two that she'd borrowed from Mark and Claire, to create the precise lighting that she wanted for the photographs. Patricia had been at her side all morning, unusually quiet, yet excessively contemplative of Magnolia. She could tell by the way she looked at her that a maelstrom of assessment was going on in her mind.

'So... it went well with Nathan after I left?' Magnolia asked, tweaking the angle of one of the lamps.

'Oh, so *now* you want to know?' Patricia responded exasperatedly. 'You didn't want to hear about it earlier.'

'Only because you said that you went on to talk about me. I don't want to hear what you said about me.'

Patricia rolled her eyes. A shadow fell across the floor, disrupting Magnolia's scene-setting and quashing her chance of discovering what had happened later the night before at the shop. There was someone outside the shop door.

'Is that someone with a delivery?' Magnolia asked. She was fiddling with her camera settings and didn't want to lose her concentration.

Patricia bobbed gracefully over to the shop front window and peered outside. 'It's Nathan. Please can he come in?'

'Oh, for God's sake!' Magnolia allowed the camera to drop from her hands, causing it to swing around her neck on its strap instead. She glared at Patricia, who gazed back at her imploringly. With a sigh of resignation, she stomped over to the door and yanked it open, almost hitting the camera with the doorknob.

'I'm only letting you come in because your mum asked me to,' she announced, lips pursed and eyes flashing as she moved aside for him to enter.

He managed to look simultaneously impressed and regretful. 'Wow, it's like an enchanting otherworld in here,' he marvelled, turning on the spot to take in the full effect of the artistically displayed abundance of chocolate treats that Magnolia had spent the morning arranging on the shelves.

'Thanks. Glad you like it,' Magnolia responded snippily. 'I'm trying to take promotional photographs, so can you and Patricia please go in the kitchen and let me get on with it? You're standing where I need to be.'

'I was hoping I could talk to you, actually,' he responded softly. 'I'm so sorry, Magnolia. For the way I spoke to you yesterday… for not believing you. I was so wrong… but these are exceptional circumstances, surely you can see that? Surely paranormal activity — especially involving my mother — gives me a little bit of leeway for forgiveness?'

'I suppose so,' Magnolia conceded. 'It was a lot for you to take in. You're forgiven.'

She gave a small smile, noticing Patricia execute a joyful somersault in mid-air in her peripheral vision. Nathan obviously noticed too; his mouth dropped open. 'Elderly acrobatics is a fairly new development for her,' Magnolia declared, deadpan. 'She's honed her repertoire of skills over the past few weeks.'

'Right… I see.' Nathan squeezed the point between his eyes with thumb and forefinger, as though trying to maintain his grip on reality. 'So… I was hoping you might let me take you out for dinner?' he asked, now focusing completely on Magnolia.

'Thanks, but I can't,' she responded softly, her smile turning sad. 'I really don't have the time at the moment, with everything that needs to be done here.'

She thought she'd meant it when she'd told him she'd forgiven him, but a sense of crushing disappointment still prevailed. Did that mean that she hadn't forgiven him, after all? Either way, she couldn't afford to expend her energy on precipitous romantic notions right now. A bubble had burst.

'OK, I understand,' Nathan replied. The sad smile seemed to be infectious. 'Is there anything I can help you with here? With no expectation whatsoever that it'll result in you having time for dinner with me at some later date?'

Patricia clapped her hands excitedly. 'You can help with the photography!'

'Who made you my business partner? I don't need any help with the photography.' Magnolia pulled the camera towards her chest defensively.

'You need more than just product shots — you need people shots, too,' Patricia advised. 'Why don't you let Nathan take a few shots of you?'

'No way,' Magnolia gripped the camera even harder. 'I like Nathan's assessment that it looks like an "enchanting otherworld" in here. If you add me to the mix, it'll spoil the whole ambiance.'

'No, it won't,' Patricia said firmly, planting herself in front of Magnolia. 'It'll *enhance* the whole ambiance. You need to tell a story. Why do you think all these artisan bakeries that are springing up have photos of cheerful bakers with their sleeves rolled up and a sparkle in their eyes adorning their promotional materials? All those images of them throwing dough around and stretching it out with enraptured looks on their faces? I've seen Jed's website, you know. That's the vibe you need.'

'She's right, you know,' Nathan contributed. 'People will want to know who weaves the magic. That gorgeous red velvet dress you're wearing will look perfect against the backdrop of the shop, and with your hair like that — sort of half-up-half-down like a waterfall — you look absolutely ethereal. Give it a chance, anyway? Let me take a few and then see how you feel?'

Magnolia's mouth twitched into a smile. 'Wow, the powerful persuasion tactics of the Daventrys. I suppose we can give it a try.'

Nathan reached out his hand, and in weird reminiscence of the day they'd met, Magnolia got the ridiculous notion he was inviting her to dance. She must have looked haughty and stand-offish, because Nathan raised an eyebrow in surprise. 'Can I have the camera, please?' he asked.

'Oh, yes, of course.' Magnolia hurriedly passed it over, then kept busy making hot chocolate whilst he took a few practice shots. Patricia sat — quietly for the time being — on a bar stool, as though she was watching a compelling production at the theatre.

'How is it that you have time for this, anyway?' Magnolia asked, finishing off the drinks and positioning herself ready for photos. 'Don't you have a job to go to?'

'I'm only working part-time at the micro-brewery… and trying to write a book the rest of the time,' Nathan replied, almost apologetically. The camera clicked as he took a photo. He reviewed it before scrutinising Magnolia anew.

'Can you flick that corkscrew curl of hair forwards?' he asked. 'It should be more prominent in the photos. It looks utterly charming.'

Magnolia gazed at him in bewilderment.

'May I?' He gestured to the front of her hair, where the loose tendrils framed her face. She nodded, and he gently, yet deftly, pulled a curl further forwards to rest against her cheek.

'It's not very hygienic to have long hair wafting around when you're making chocolate,' she grumbled.

'You're not making chocolate right now, though, are you? All the chocolate is safely packaged up ready for sale.' He grinned and clicked the camera. 'Can you tilt your chin towards the window, please? I think that's your best angle. Oh, and maybe you could lean against the counter a bit, just so that the full skirt of your dress flares out? I want a few flamboyant and dramatic shots.'

'OK.' Magnolia complied, shaking her skirt out and using one of the bar stools as a prop to maintain its fanned-out position. The camera clicked.

'What's your book about?' she asked.

'I can't tell you. Sorry, I know that sounds pretentious — I'm just a bit uptight about sharing the details. You're only the second person I've even told I'm writing a book.'

'Second and third person,' Patricia piped up.

'You're not a person, you're a ghost,' Magnolia quipped. Nathan, having turned to look at his mother, now seemed confused by her blissful connection with Magnolia's half-empty mug of hot chocolate.

'A ghost, who can smell hot chocolate... and relishes it as one of the scant transferable joys from being mortal,' Magnolia clarified for him.

'Who'd have guessed.' He gave an incredulous laugh.

'Can you at least tell us the genre?' Magnolia cajoled.

'No, I can't, sorry.'

'Well, this is highly dissatisfactory,' Patricia complained. 'I won't be around long enough to be able to read it, and you won't even give us a synopsis.'

'Oh, Hallelujah, so you are going to depart at some point soon, then,' Magnolia mock-rejoiced, moving to stand against a backdrop of chocolate gingerbread stars at Nathan's bidding. The camera clicked.

'Marvellously moody shot,' Nathan declared.

Magnolia continued to address Patricia. 'I had visions of a dystopian future, a hundred years from now, where this place is razed to the ground by sugar protestors who've taken over the world, and there's no one left for miles around except you, wandering around the wreckage.'

'Damn, that's my book plot.' Nathan slapped his forehead theatrically, and Patricia let out a great cackle. Magnolia laughed too, throwing her head back joyfully without inhibition, and Nathan took a flurry of photos. Then her head snapped to the door, and he drew away from the camera.

A woman and child stood on the threshold. The child incongruously looked smarter than the woman, in a little corduroy suit jacket with shiny conker-coloured shoes that matched his shiny conker-coloured hair. The woman wore a pinafore dress over purple tights, and her hair was like a dandelion clock; there was a look of astonishment on her face.

'Beth!' Magnolia cried; then surreptitiously muttered at Patricia under her breath, 'Why don't you ever close the door properly?' She rushed forward to greet the unexpected visitors with hugs.

'Sorry to drop in unannounced', Beth said. 'We were in the area anyway, doing some Christmas shopping and Dominic was desperate to see what your shop looked like. I told him he had to wait until the opening day, but... anyway, I can see that you're obviously busy with...' Uncharacteristically flustered, she lost her words, eyes flitting in disbelief between the wonders of the shop, the radiant Magnolia and the mystery man with the camera. Dominic had stepped into the centre of the shop and was drinking in the magic of its wares with silent awe. She motioned for him to return to her side.

'No, it's OK,' Magnolia said hurriedly. 'Stay for a drink? My skulking robot does tea and coffee as well as hot chocolate.'

Dumbfounded, Beth looked at Nathan.

'I don't mean *him*, I mean *that*!' Magnolia gestured towards her brass vintage-style drinks machine.

'No, you're obviously having a private moment with…'

'Nathan,' Nathan supplied helpfully with a grin.

'…Nathan,' Beth continued. 'And we really don't want to get in the way of a romantic liaison, so…'

'Romantic liaison? Beth, since when have you used words like that?' Magnolia cried exasperatedly. 'Look, we're just taking promotional photos for the shop. And we're hardly going to be having a "romantic liaison" with his mother present, are we?'

Everyone paused.

'Whose mother?' Beth asked, looking around in confusion.

'Damn,' Magnolia cursed quietly through gritted teeth. Patricia's infamous cackle rang out once again, and Nathan's shoulders shook with mirth as he looked at the floor in an effort to suppress it.

'Nathan's mother; she's just gone to get some sandwiches from the deli, but she'll be back soon.'

'Wow, you're spectacular at digging yourself into a hole!' Patricia exclaimed. 'Now what are you going to say if they stay, when I don't come back from the deli? Not to mention the fact that I'm dead; what if she discovers that little nugget later on?'

Thankfully, the day somehow unfurled from then onwards without any further drama. Nathan feigned a phone call from his mother — apparently, she'd "taken a funny turn" at the deli and just wanted him to take her home for a lie-down — so he calmly departed, leaving Magnolia to catch up with her guests, whilst Patricia slunk away to the outbuilding.

Dominic sat quietly, totally entranced by the giant chocolate marshmallow sprinkled with popping candy that Magnolia had given him to dunk into his hot chocolate, whilst Magnolia and Beth transferred the photos Nathan had taken to Magnolia's laptop, and flicked through them with mounting excitement.

They both agreed he was a talented photographer. He somehow managed to conjure the rich, luxurious splendour and dash of otherworldliness that Magnolia sought so fervently for her brand identity; and he managed to do it with her in the frame too. Narrowing down to a select few photos for the website and social media was a difficult but enjoyable task, which they undertook together, finishing just as dusk drew in.

'So… tell me again why you two aren't a couple?' Beth formulated this as a question, chin resting on her open palms, elbows on the counter, giving her the maximum air of attentiveness as she gazed at Magnolia.

'I didn't tell you in the first place,' Magnolia retorted.

'Oh, come on.'

Magnolia looked set to speak again, but then stopped. Mistaking her reticence for concern that Dominic might hear something that he shouldn't, Beth turned to her son. 'Dominic, sweetie, go and play with the cogs and gauges for five minutes.' She gestured towards Magnolia's shelf brackets, which was just as well, as Dominic had no idea what cogs and gauges were, so was in need of the direction.

I can hardly tell her that he was horrible and disbelieving when I told him that his mother is a ghost, Magnolia fretted.

'So what's wrong with Nathan? I can see that there's a sparkle, so why aren't you with him?'

Dominic turned from tugging at a gear to look for a sparkle instead; his eyes flitting around the shop expectantly.

'It's just… the timing's wrong. I need to focus on the shop for now.'

'And then when you want him, he won't be there anymore.'

'Well, that's just tough luck, isn't it?'

Beth's head dropped to the counter with exaggerated dismay.

At the shop door, just as they were about to go their separate ways — Dominic was rubbing his eyes and mumbling about a promised toad-in-the-hole for tea — Beth grabbed Magnolia's face in her palms in her typically tactile manner and stared into her eyes.

'Just so that you know — I don't believe for a moment that you and Nathan are just friends,' she declared firmly. Magnolia opened her mouth to respond, but Beth released her face and flapped a hand dismissively. 'Don't bother saying anything. I won't believe you.' And with a triumphant gleam in her eyes and the blowing of a kiss, she then departed with Dominic in tow.

Chapter Twenty-Eight

Magnolia clapped her hands in delight when Sophie arrived at the shop for the chocolate sampling promotion. 'You look amazing!' she enthused. As well as the cute red coat with appliqué Christmas tree detail that Claire had previously mentioned, Sophie's bouncy hair was in bunches tied with matching Christmas-tree-patterned ribbons, and her patent leather shoes had a glittery-red sparkle.

'It was supposed to snow,' Sophie declared indignantly, looking around at the sky and the pavement. Magnolia looked questioningly at Claire, who shrugged and smiled.

'It wasn't in the forecast; I suppose she just thought it'd be appropriate, and the thought somehow morphed into expectation.'

Sophie sighed theatrically.

'Well, I'm glad that it's not snowing,' Magnolia said. 'Because if it was, you'd want to be out sledging down the hills, or having snowball fights, and I wouldn't have you here helping me.'

Sophie looked troubled. 'Couldn't I do all of it?'

'Well, you couldn't do all of it at the same time, could you? But that's why it's good that it isn't snowing at the moment; because now you don't have to decide what you'd prefer to do.'

And now, bizarrely, I feel like I'm a wicked witch who's banished the snow solely to prevent children from having fun, so that I can use them as slave labour instead.

'Anyway, I need to dash, if that's alright,' Claire said. 'I can't let this prime opportunity to shop for Christmas stuff pass me by.'

Once they were positioned with their goodies, it didn't take long for the two On Yer Bike mechanics to make an appearance.

'Wow, look at those!' Gavin said, his pitch rising with excitement as he rubbed his hands.

'They look stonking,' Tilly contributed. She had a rogue piece of handlebar tape stuck to her wrist.

'You can't have any,' Sophie said crossly, shooing them away.

'Why not?'

'Because you're the wrong people.'

''She means that you already know what my chocolates taste like,' Magnolia clarified. 'The whole point of the exercise is to tempt people who haven't tried them yet.'

'We haven't tried *these* particular chocolates.'

'Yeah, plus we're setting the right scene; if people see that you've got a crowd around you, they'll be more interested in finding out what's going on.'

'Let them have one each, Soph,' Magnolia instructed. 'But you know the deal,' she said — turning back to address Gavin and Tilly. 'You have to tell your customers how fantastic my chocolates are at every opportunity.'

'Yeah, you know the deal,' Sophie repeated, with gangster-like gravitas, her eyes narrowed. Spluttering on their chocolate, they both stifled a giggle feigning fear instead.

'Yes, miss,' they agreed, before returning to the bike shop.

An hour in, and Magnolia and Sophie had had lots of enthusiastic recipients of their chocolate tasters, with many people wanting to make a purchase there and then. Maybe Magnolia had slipped up on that one; she'd gone with a "building up anticipation" angle instead. Sophie drew the crowds like a magnet, and Magnolia allowed her to eat one chocolate for every fifteen or so that she gave out.

The only dodgy moment came when Sophie tried to offer a chocolate to a Labrador, and Magnolia had to explain that dogs shouldn't eat chocolate, because it makes them very sick. Both Sophie and the Labrador seemed rather disgruntled, but the owner was appreciative of the restraint, and even announced her intention to visit the shop the following week to buy a chocolate box as a Christmas gift for each of her seven grandchildren.

'Are you OK, sweetie?' Magnolia asked, as a lull from the crowds settled over them. 'Not too cold?'

'Yep,' Sophie responded. *It serves me right for asking two questions at once*, Magnolia thought wryly. 'I like watching different people walk,' her niece elaborated. Then she tilted her head to one side quizzically. 'Why isn't that posh old lady helping us?'

'Which posh old lady?'

'The posh old lady in your shop. Has she forgotten her coat?'

Magnolia was astonished. 'Did you see someone in the shop today?'

Sophie had shoved a white chocolate honeycomb snowball into her mouth at the same time Magnolia asked the question. She attempted to answer with her mouth popping full, and Magnolia feared a spray of honeycomb would shoot from her nose. 'It's OK, wait until you've finished that,' she said hurriedly.

On tenterhooks, she waited. The attention span of a four-year-old being especially short, however, once the chocolate was eaten, Sophie had completely forgotten what she was saying, and instead began scrutinising a leaf stuck in a spider's web against the shop's exterior wall as it fluttered in the breeze. Her tray of chocolates dipped alarmingly, and Magnolia reached out to steady it.

'Who did you see in the shop today, Soph?' she coaxed.

'An old lady wearing purple clothes. But she walked like a not-old lady. She talked to you, but she didn't talk to me. But sometimes grown-ups don't talk to me, because I'm just a kid and I don't say sensible things.'

'Was it when we were putting the chocolates on the trays?'

'Yep. And she talked to you, but you didn't talk back to her. Isn't that being rude, Auntie Nolly?'

'Well… it's not being rude if I didn't hear her.'

'I think you did hear her,' Sophie declared emphatically.

Magnolia was just trying to formulate her response, when Jed ventured out of the bakery to see what was going on. He promptly declared that he wasn't keen on chocolate when Sophie offered one to him, then took one anyway. A look of dawning realisation crossed his face. It seemed he did like chocolate, after all.

He offered to swap a couple of loaves of bread for any leftovers. When there weren't any, he gave Magnolia the bread anyway; a tear and share pumpkin and sage *focaccia* and a sourdough loaf. Magnolia gave the vegetable-infused one to Sophie, but she was adamant that it needed to be converted into soldiers to accompany her tea-time dippy-egg. When Jed explained that you couldn't really toast soldiers in advance, which would be tricky with *focaccia* anyway, she was rather perturbed and decided she didn't want the loaf after all. So Magnolia took both.

'Sophie can see you,' Magnolia announced breathlessly, as she finally pushed into the shop, once their work was done. Having successfully charmed an impressive procession of passers-by with her chocolate offerings, Sophie had now been whisked away by Claire, before any further paranormal encounters or tricky conversations could take place.

Patricia looked up from the hot chocolate counter; she was sat on a stool, trying to make two coffee beans collide, but they kept zooming past each other. Magnolia noticed a few smashed up casualties heaped against the wall — evidence that she'd been practicing her technique for some time. 'Ooo, really? That's interesting,' Patricia responded with relish, the beans forgotten.

'It's not a good development,' Magnolia said, sighing as she sank onto the stool next to Patricia. 'What's going to happen when the shop opens? Imagine if all the children can see you and they all start chattering away to their parents about you — half of them will probably be excited, the other half traumatised — all pointing at you and asking if you're Mrs Claus, or… the devil, or something.'

'Well, that's an impressive transition — from Mrs Claus to the devil.'

'I'm just trying to anticipate the full spectrum of possibility.'

'Well, you don't need to worry, because I'll be gone by then.'

'Will you really? If you say so.' Magnolia moved to the kitchen and began filling the sink. Patricia played with the coffee beans a little longer and then drifted into the kitchen as well.

'Oh, Magnolia?' Magnolia looked up from washing the chocolate taster trays. 'She spoke to me when you were putting the bins outside. She asked if I was a ghost. I didn't answer. She then told me that she'd been stargazing in the moors two nights ago with her dad, and she'd seen Jupiter and Saturn, as well as lots of twinkly little stars. She said they were much better than me.'

The dishcloth fell from Magnolia's hand with a plop. 'What did you say to her then?'

'I thought you'd want me to just ignore her, so that's what I did.'

'Good. Oh, my God. Well... at least she wasn't scared of you. Let's hope all the other extraordinary things going on in her life mean that she forgets about you.'

Chapter Twenty-Nine

Six rewarding yet exhausting days passed at the shop, and before Magnolia knew it, it was the eve of her shop opening day. She'd heard nothing from Nathan since messaging him to thank him profusely for his photography. He'd responded graciously within the half hour, but that was all — nothing in the days since. Magnolia felt deeply disappointed; surprisingly so.

She'd taken on two part-time assistants — Claire, plus an enthusiastic and conscientious twenty-two-year-old called Justin, who also worked part-time at the bakery. In several years' time he wanted to open his own restaurant; until then, he wanted to build up as much relevant experience as possible. Jed had only been able to offer him twenty hours' work per week, and with Magnolia offering the same shift pattern to Claire, he slotted neatly into the other twenty-hour period that she wanted to fill.

She locked up the shop and stepped into the street. Shop windows spilled festive cheer all around: mince pies, stollen and Yule logs from the bakery — the latter had actually been made by Magnolia, at Jed's suggestion — and he was selling it on her behalf; poinsettias, holly, mistletoe and rich-coloured bouquets

273

from the florist; plump turkeys from the butcher's. The toy shop was a riot of colour and Christmas excitement, and unusually yet effectively, even the optician's window featured a Christmas tree decorated with spectacles in place of baubles.

She felt a little swell of pride as she drew level with the window of Mark's bike shop; a couple of evenings ago she'd raided his workshop for unwanted cogs and gears yet again — this time, for his benefit. She'd found a three-foot-long metal pole and stacked the cogs and gears in order of decreasing circumference, creating a cone shape which looked pleasingly like a Christmas tree once she'd added a star to the top and some sparkly adornments.

The air carried the scent of roast chestnuts, and Magnolia saw with delight that the grocers were roasting them at a little cart just outside their shop door. She couldn't resist buying a bag of them, splitting the shells open impatiently whilst they were still rather hot to eat their earthy yet sweet centres.

Two teenage girls with novelty reindeer antler headbands passed by, clutching at each other as they laughed, their long, winter coats flapping loose to reveal short, sequinned party dresses. One of the girl's coats hung unevenly on one side from the tell-tale weight of the glass liquor bottle Magnolia could just about see. They reminded her of herself and Beth at seventeen, and she smiled in fond memory, hoping they'd enjoy the pleasant buzz of just a little naughty indulgence, without taking it too far and getting completely wasted.

As she entered the park, she saw the council had strung Christmas lights on the trees; tiny, tasteful silvery-white lights dressing previously austere branches gloriously, a respite from their harsh nakedness between the fiery splendour of autumn and the spring rebirth.

She quickened her pace, with thoughts of fleecy slipper boots, a leftover wedge of *spanakopita* and the wonderfully intriguing book she was reading.

As she turned into her street and approached her little terraced house, she noticed something on her doorstep. It was only when she actually arrived at her door that she realised what it was: a large jar of sherbet lemons. Rendered immobile through disbelief, she just stared at it for a few seconds. There was a note taped to the top of the lid: *Tip me out, but not in the bin.*

Unlocking the door, the jar under her arm, she went straight through to the kitchen, unscrewed the lid, and poured the boiled sweets out onto the kitchen table. Several skittered across the surface and onto the floor, but Magnolia didn't notice, her attention caught by the bar of chocolate that had been hidden within, now unearthed. It was an old-fashioned bar of chocolate; a foil-encased flat rectangle wrapped further in a paper sleeve, depicting a dark chocolate slab snapped in half and oozing with mint fondant. The exact type of chocolate bar she'd coveted as a child — and told Nathan about in the park.

Where on earth did you find one of these, Nathan? she marvelled; turning the now largely obsolete confection over in her hands and scrutinising its detail. She slid the bar free of its paper sheath and peeled back the silver foil. The fresh, peppy scent of mint danced with the rich, cocoa punch of dark chocolate. Noticing a small slip of card slotted between the bar and the foil, she withdrew it to read in gold, loopy writing:

Good luck for tomorrow. You deserve all the sweetness in life that your heart desires. X

It was the most insightful, enchanting gesture anyone had ever reached out to her with. She shivered with the sudden sense that she was on the edge of a "before" and "after" moment; that the decisions she was to make in the next twenty-four hours would profoundly determine the course of the rest of her life.

She sat in quiet contemplation as the minutes ticked by, her stomach growling for *spanakopita* and her feet growing chilly for their slipper boots unheeded, whilst her heart soared. It was time for her to stop behaving like a complete idiot.

Her phone buzzed. Several people had contacted her to wish her luck for the next day, which was lovely, but before she knew it, it was way past the time she'd usually be eating dinner. Her mum kindly yet wrongly informed her that she needed to take a bath to relax. She'd long ago given up telling Lauren that she didn't take baths, she always took showers — yet most Christmases and birthdays she still received wonderfully fragranced yet totally redundant bath oils or salts from her. It seemed such a shame to waste them; Magnolia decided that she'd fill the kitchen sink with hot water and one of the scented treats next time she sat at the kitchen table to work or read. That way, she'd still benefit from them.

Car doors slammed outside, and there was a dual cascade of gentle laughter before the joyful tripping of heels on asphalt. Seemingly, the neighbours were enjoying themselves.

Suddenly, Magnolia's courage began to dwindle. Should she phone him? Text him? In the end, she did neither, purely because she had no idea what to say. She couldn't even process how she felt about him. She needed to concentrate on finishing her preparations for the shop opening. She couldn't allow herself to be distracted by a man at this moment in time.

She opened her action plan spreadsheet and placed golden ticks in the neat boxes against the last few items. Then she retrieved the dress she wanted to wear the next day from her wardrobe, checked it hadn't mysteriously acquired creases during its time therein, and hung it on the back of her bedroom door, just in case she had a brain freeze in the morning and completely forgot which dress she'd decided upon.

She did, however, put the gift and note on her bedside table — and looked at them far too many times in between reading her book, before attempting to sleep.

A few minutes after switching her light off she flipped it back on again. She really should respond in some way. "Thanks for the gift", she finally texted him; without any kisses.

An hour later, the night was nudging her malevolently.

Half of her wanted to spin forwards in time to a point beyond the shop opening day; to a point when her every decision and action didn't feel imbued with such significance regarding her fundamental future. The other half wanted to screech to a halt and reverse to a point before she'd invested so much hope and energy — and yes, money — into her dream; to be ensconced somewhere safer and inconsequential, where she could just live her life in a quiet haze of ignorant detachment.

The entirety of her being, at that moment, wanted Nathan to disappear from her fevered thoughts completely. His effect was as disruptive as gin fizz pouring onto a bed of ice.

Chapter Thirty

The launch of Cocomolioco was to be an all-day event. Magnolia had baked two large batches each of chocolate brownies, millionaires' shortbread and chocolate gingerbread as free treats for potential customers and had just begun displaying them on tall copper cake stands under great glass domes. Free hot chocolate as well as coffee and tea were also on offer. Hundreds of tiny white fairy lights had been artfully strung wherever there was space, and she'd hired Jessie, a friend of a friend, to sing seasonal songs and play acoustic guitar.

There were going to be three hour-long chocolate decorating workshops throughout the day; late morning, early afternoon and late afternoon. Whilst Magnolia wanted to give an insight into her craft, teaching dozens of people — many of them likely to be children — how to temper chocolate seemed far too overwhelming a feat, so instead, she'd made over a hundred chocolate Father Christmases, reindeer and snowmen, all ready to be decorated in the workshops with coloured icing, jelly sweets, crispy chocolate beads and a cornucopia of other cheerful and tasty adornments.

Having regretfully decided she didn't have space in the shop for a Christmas tree, Magnolia had been delighted when Claire turned up brandishing an adorable four-foot-tall Fraser fir; fully confident that they'd somehow make it fit. They realised that if they made the hot chocolate counter temporarily standing-room only, they'd be able to slot the tree quite neatly where the stools were.

Being short of the required quantity of Victorian baubles and trinkets to adorn the tree — the theme was important — Magnolia promptly caramelised a fresh batch of orange slices, half-dipped them in white chocolate, and sprinkled them with edible gold. Not only did they look perfect alongside the few decorations she did have, but they emanated a scrumptious scent, which mingled magnificently with the natural oils of the fir.

Even the reproduction Louis XIV chair had been given an outing. It looked pleasingly festive, and seeing as Nathan hadn't yet claimed it, Magnolia thought it would be perfect as a chair for Jess to sit on as she played the guitar.

She'd just arranged the generous wedges of millionaires' shortbread to her liking when the tiny bell above the shop door tinkled. She turned around — remembering just in time not to wipe her sticky hands on her lustrous midnight-blue silk dress — to see Nathan in the doorway.

'I just wondered whether you needed a hand with the launch,' he said sheepishly.

She shrugged nonchalantly, trying to ignore the thump of her heart. 'Patricia floated up the walls to hang the highest fairy lights, so I don't need you for that.'

He stepped forward. 'Well... maybe I hoped you might need me for something else.'

She made an exaggerated show of thinking, forefinger held to the corner of her mouth. 'I've hired a singer-slash-acoustic guitarist, so I don't need you for ambiance.'

'Well... I hoped you might need me for this.'

In a blur, his lips were on hers, and something changed within Magnolia forever; some exquisite soaring of the soul. It was deliciously passionate, his hands clasping her face as he kissed her with intensity, before a lighter playfulness and then back again.

'I suppose I do need you for that,' Magnolia whispered dreamily as they broke apart, gazing at each other.

'Yeah, I thought so.'

She pushed him playfully in the chest. He stumbled back a step as they both gave a short giggle. 'Oh, no! Now you've got a sort of caramel handprint on your shirt. I was just about to wash my hands when you came in. Sorry, you can't seem to come in here without getting all clarted up.'

'Damn, I knew it was a mistake coming here. This shirt meant the world to me,' Nathan joked, before continuing gently with, 'In the grand scheme of things,

I think we can safely say the shirt was worth sacrificing, don't you think?'

'Do you think Patricia saw us?' Magnolia suddenly considered aloud, a little embarrassed. 'We might have scared her off to the outbuilding!'

Nathan laughed as he strode into the kitchen, Magnolia on his heels. 'Mum?' he called.

There was no sign of her.

'I knew it… she's escaped to the outbuilding in disgust.'

'I think she's gone, Nolly,' Nathan said gently. 'Like… really gone. Crossed over. I think this was what she was waiting for.'

'She can't have gone… she didn't say goodbye.' In anguish, Magnolia rushed to the back door, but Nathan quickly yet gently pulled her back, pointing towards the kettle. Secured under the kettle base, a piece of paper fluttered in the breeze whipped up by Magnolia's sudden movement. She stilled, and locked onto Nathan's gaze. Tentatively approaching the sheet of paper, she retrieved it. It was a note — a beam of low winter sun illuminating each word.

Dearest Magnolia,

I'm sorry for using your Madagascan vanilla extract pen to write this. I know it was very expensive and is only intended for decorating chocolate with. I couldn't see a normal pen, and there wasn't much time to look for one, as I could feel the call from above getting stronger.

So, I think we all know why I didn't cross over until now. I was waiting for you and Nathan to realise there was something special between you worth taking a chance on. I'm so delighted that the two people I love most in the world have found each other — but don't let that be a shackle around you. If it doesn't work out, don't be daft enough to stay together just because of me. Just give it a chance.

I wish you great joy and success with your chocolate shop; I hope it's everything you want it to be. You really are an excellent chocolatier.

Thank you for such warm companionship during my ghost-phase.

Your loving friend, Patricia

Hiccupping on a laugh and a sob, Magnolia passed the note to Nathan, a slow smile of acknowledgment eventually tugging at her lips. It was pure Patricia. And it was the perfect way for them to part.

As he finished reading the note, Nathan smiled knowingly. Did that merely mean that he recognised his mother and her motivations in every word, or did it also mean that he wanted to explore what she had suggested therein? Magnolia didn't know; she only knew that she wanted him to kiss her again.

He handed the note back to her, and she folded it neatly to a quarter of the size before slipping it into her dress pocket. His eyes lingered on hers, before he sighed regretfully and inched backwards a little.

'Whilst I'd really love to know whether that kiss meant what I hope it did… and I really can't believe I'm saying this…I think opening your chocolate shop is more important right now. I can see an anxious-looking woman with a guitar at the shop door, and there's a throng of kids bouncing around, pressing their faces against the windows.'

'Oh, God, I know. I need to focus.' Magnolia's expression changed from dreamy to one of determination. She quickly checked her appearance in the reflective splash-back behind the hob, smoothing her hair, before proceeding towards the shop door. Turning around halfway, she returned to Nathan. She drew his face to hers with both hands and planted a quick yet tender kiss on his lips.

'It definitely meant something,' she whispered, reluctantly breaking away and smiling at him beatifically. 'You could come back at closing time and we could talk over a drink? I'll crack open the new bottle of cognac that I'm supposed to be saving for chocolate-making.'

Nathan laughed. 'That sounds great, but I could stay instead, and help you charm the incoming stampede if you want me to?'

'That would be perfect.'

Before unlocking the front door, Magnolia paused to savour this pivotal moment; looking all around at the bounteous shelves.

Slabs of cheerful traditional treats — coconut ice, peanut brittle, raspberry ripple fudge and maple honeycomb, all generously dunked in thick white, milk or dark chocolate — contrasted beautifully with sophisticated cognac, champagne or ginger wine truffles. Delicate chocolate-dipped meringues, some flavoured with cinnamon, coffee or strawberry, were neatly displayed alongside mini chocolate spheres encasing liquid caramel married with spiced fig, Cornish smoked sea salt or bergamot. There was also shelf space for various flavours of *feuillantine* and caramelised macadamia, pecan, almond and cashew nuts — all liberally coated with chocolate.

Magnolia could guess which goodies would be most popular with children — her three-D chocolate gift boxes with their surprise fillings of chocolate enrobed popcorn, fruit jellies and mini marshmallows had come together wonderfully. They looked particularly joyful as they nestled against chocolate lollipops and figurines shaped like snowmen, Father Christmas, angels and reindeer.

She finally opened the door. The pavement beyond was overflowing with people. Family, friends and fellow small business owners she'd met along the way peppered the throng; but amongst these familiar faces were many more she didn't recognise, smiles wide and eyes bright, framed as they were by cheery bobble-hats and twisting scarves.

She welcomed them in and they spilled forth, parents attempting to restrain their rapturous children with varying degrees of success, whilst poor Jessie tried to hurry towards the area Magnolia had prepared for her alongside the Christmas tree without bashing anyone with her guitar case in the process.

It was everything Magnolia had been waiting for.

Epilogue

Bruges in the depths of winter was a cornucopia of enchantment on a whole new level for Magnolia, who'd only ever seen the city during a golden summer. She found the medieval streets to be at their best when plunged into the drama of inky-black nights with their theatrical, looming shadows, and bright-white, snow-shrouded days.

Leaving the shop just five weeks after opening wasn't as crazy as some might think. December had been a bumper month, more profitable than Magnolia had anticipated; January was generally the quietest month for chocolate sales, and Claire had proved herself to be a remarkable shop manager. Magnolia was even teaching her how to temper chocolate. Plus, Magnolia wanted to pay her respects to Agnes as soon as possible, having missed the funeral due to Mathias' fury towards her.

The magic of Bruges was also enhanced by the sparkling company. Nathan had come with her on the three-day trip, and whilst she tried not to make comparisons with Mathias, she couldn't help marvelling at Nathan's wonder and enthusiasm, which matched her own and added lustre to her second visit to the city.

The first night, they fell upon the sleigh bed in their hotel room before the snowflakes on their outer garments had even melted away; dozens of passionate kisses full of promise leading to this moment. Their limbs tumbled together deliciously and inevitably, squeezing and yielding, dreamy and smooth yet jagged and hyper-real, fervent and languorous and back again, extraordinary and unusual yet somehow achingly familiar. All-consuming.

The next morning, reluctantly disentangling her limbs from Nathan's, Magnolia went out in search of coffee and breakfast pastries; hurrying back to burrow beneath the bedcovers with him once again.

He was sat up against the headboard, scribbling furiously in his notebook. The early morning light stretching through the medieval windowpane cast a diamond pattern all over his bare chest and loosely covered legs as he wrote, transforming him into a bewitching *commedia dell'arte* harlequin.

Magnolia couldn't resist reaching forwards to kiss his lips, then whispered an apology, as she realised he'd probably think she was trying to sneak a peek at his writing; having suffered a recent writing drought he'd suddenly been struck by inspiration and written a flurry of new pages. He didn't mind, though; he angled the notebook towards her invitingly as he plucked a croissant from the paper bag beside them and tore at it with his teeth, sending pastry flakes scattering.

His story was exquisite and beguiling. It was wholly unexpected in genre and setting — insofar as the double-page spread just revealed to Magnolia could be taken as representative of the entire novel — yet not in style; that was quintessentially Nathan and therefore unsurprisingly extraordinary. She told him so, and his eyes lit up with the compliment.

They finally emerged from the hotel at around eleven o' clock. Their first stop was the *crêperie*, and whilst it inevitably wasn't the same without Agnes and Frederick, the new owners had changed remarkably little about the place. As they sat sharing a platter of crepes with chocolate sauce and whipped cream, spirals of steam dancing from their accompanying mugs of coffee, Magnolia was delighted to see a large, framed photograph prominently displayed above the payment counter. It was Agnes as a bright-eyed young woman, holding aloft a jug of melted chocolate, a colossal stack of crepes in front of her awaiting the cascade. Frederick had his arms wrapped around her from behind and was planting a kiss on the side of her neck. It exuded such joy, love and playfulness that Magnolia's breath hitched in her throat.

After a few hours of wonderful wandering, as twilight softly closed in, they stopped at a florist. The crowds were congregating in the *markt*, attracted by the ice-skating and mulled wine stalls, which endured into these first couple of new-year weeks. It meant Agnes' favourite humpbacked bridge was delightfully quiet.

Magnolia spent a few moments in peaceful contemplation and memory of her friend and mentor, before casting a single yellow rose into the water running beneath. Two huge snowflakes settled on the upturned petals as the rose bobbed serenely on its way, and a passing swan seemed to gaze at it reverentially.

Once she motioned that she was ready to move on, Nathan, having stood beside her the whole time, drew her into a comforting embrace and kissed the top of her head. She knew he'd be thinking about Patricia, as she now was too. Her life had become so much richer having known both women, and despite missing them terribly, she felt determined to live her life to the full; to cherish love and to have the courage to push her chocolate business to its full potential.

'What would you like to do next?' Nathan asked, as they wandered away from the bridge, their feet imprinting the feather-soft fresh snow that was just beginning to lay on the cobbles.

Magnolia smiled blissfully. For the first time ever, she felt that the myriad of things that she wanted to do next were delightfully in her grasp.